Bullet Through the Art

A Sam Gordon Cozy Mystery

Anne Seidel

Bullet Through the Art

Copyright © 2023 by Anne Seidel

Cover design by DLR Cover Designs

ISBN: 978-1-962667-00-5

This book is lovingly dedicated to the memory of my father, Kendall R. Seidel. An autodidact, bibliophile and artist, whose love of learning, art and adventure through books, and in life, definitely influenced me. I know he'd be over the moon that I've embarked on this journey and that I've found a home for all my storytelling.

I love you Dad!

Acknowledgements

I absolutely must acknowledge my family and friends, who've listened to me drone on about my stories and everything I've been learning about – for years. Thank you so much for your support, patience, indulgence and encouragement.

To the extraordinary women of 1667, I could not have done any of this without you. The sharing of knowledge, experiences-from beginner to seasoned writer, the sprints, plot parties and encouragement... are priceless. From the bottom of this Killer Dame's heart, I thank you!

I love you ALL!

Contents

Chapter One

Samantha "Sam" Gordon stepped out of the rental car. It was dusk, and the air was cool on her skin. She inhaled the sweet aroma of orange blossoms. The sign read No Parking 10 AM - 8 PM on Sundays. She checked her smartwatch. 7:45. Close enough. She looked up at the familiar sign for her aunt's art and craft store, All Souls Art & Craft Studio. The memory of many days after school spent at the studio came rushing back.

It was dark inside. Sam glanced at her watch again. The studio should still be open. The windows, usually displaying paintings, ceramics, or other artwork from the students, were draped off so she couldn't see the inside of the studio from the sidewalk. Her hand gripped the shiny brass doorknob, but it was locked. Sam pulled her phone out, but before she could hit redial, she heard noises coming from inside. She leaned in and pressed her ear to the door.

"Grab the other end of the pole." A male voice she didn't recognize.

"Shhh! She'll be here any minute!" A female voice she knew all too well.

Sam stood back and grinned like the Grinch before he stole Christmas. She scurried around the corner to the back of the studio. Gently twisting the knob of the back door, it clicked open. *Unlocked*. Sam chastised Aunt Lily in her head as she quietly eased the door open.

The only light in the rear of the studio came from the table lamp on the office desk. She hugged the wall as she made her way to the studio. Just before she reached the opening, she paused and swiped her phone on to video, and pressed the red record button. She felt around for the light switch on the wall, suppressed a giggle that nearly escaped, then flipped the light switch and yelled.

"Gotcha!"

Screams and shrieks were all she heard as confetti flew out of someone's hand, and a room full of startled people bumped into each other as they twisted around to face her, their faces a mix of terror and laughter. And she caught it all on video.

Sam laughed. "Sorry. I couldn't resist."

Aunt Lily fluttered through the crowd and into the center. "Samantha, we were supposed to surprise *you*!"

Sam rushed into her aunt's open arms. They squeezed each other so tightly they looked like a human cylinder.

Aunt Lily stepped back and studied her niece. "You look wonderful! I can't wait to hear all about everything, but first, your welcome home party!"

Sam turned to the party goers with barely enough time to focus on their faces before Aunt Lily addressed the room.

"Attention, everyone! Thank you for coming to welcome home my beloved, and mischievous, niece, Samantha Gordon!" Lily raised her glass, and the guests followed. "It is so wonderful to have you home. Cheers!"

"Woo hoo! Cheers! Welcome home, Sam!" The guests toasted Sam.

Sam blushed and looked at the well-wishers, a little embarrassed by the fuss. Only recognizing a few faces, she guessed most of the guests were her aunt's friends. It didn't feel like it had been that long since

Sam had been home, but it was clearly long enough her aunt thought it was worthy of a party.

"She's been on cloud nine all week," a familiar voice came from behind.

Sam spun around. "Joan, it's so great to see you." She hugged Joan Harris, Aunt Lily's friend and the manager for the art studio. "I hope Aunt Lily hasn't talked about me so much you're sick of me before I even arrived."

"Never. She's so thrilled you're going to be helping with the fair." Joan squeezed Sam's arm.

"She is getting around well. She may not even need my help." Sam watched her aunt move about with barely a limp.

"She's definitely loving the new soft cast, but she still does more than she should, and it's good––" Joan stopped abruptly. Sam followed her gaze to a crowd by the entrance, but didn't see anything unusual. "It's good you're here." Joan patted Sam's forearm. "I better move those appetizers. Enjoy yourself." She scampered off.

Before Sam could decide her next move, strong arms wrapped around her waist from behind, lifted her into the air, swung around and planted her in front of a tall curly-headed blonde woman, hands on hips standing in front of her.

"Girl, you're the guest of honor, so I forgive you for not calling me the second you landed."

Sam beamed at the sight of her best friend. "I was––oomph!" Her words got squeezed out of her as she found herself sandwiched between her two best friends, Suzanne Quinlan aka Q and Greg Farina, the one who had twirled her around. It was a true love human sandwich. Sam and Q had met in junior high and had been best friends ever since. Then she'd met Greg in her first year at college and they'd got on like a house on fire. Never a romance, just a great friendship.

She'd tried her hand at matchmaking between Q and Greg, and she wasn't wrong. It was love at first sight for the two of them, and they'd been together ever since.

"I can't breathe," Sam said hoarsely as Q and Greg whooped and hollered. "You guys."

"Just one more squeeze." Q squeezed one last time before she and Greg released her.

Sam whirled around so she could see Greg face to face and wrapped her arms around his neck, giving him a quick kiss on the cheek.

"Don't get jealous, honey," Greg teased Q.

"Puh-leeze, that's why she introduced you to me. She wasn't interested," Q quipped back.

Sam hooked an arm with each one on either side of her. "I love you both. I'm so happy you're here!" Sam pulled them in with a little shimmy.

"We weren't sure you'd remember us now that you're famous!" Q mocked with a fake Southern drawl.

"Famous? What are you talking about?" Sam asked.

Q pointed to an easel with a large copy of a photo Sam had submitted to a regional magazine photo contest when she was living and working in Spain and won.

Sam blushed. "Oh my gosh. I wish Aunt Lily wouldn't make such a fuss. It was a local photo contest for *Vamos! Espana*, not National Geographic or Time Life." Sam looked around for Aunt Lily.

"She's so proud of you, hon," Q said.

"Small magazine or not, it's a great photo, Sam," Greg said.

Sam took in the sight of the cobblestone street in Alhambra at sunset. The sun peeked through the trees, looking like one of the lanterns illuminating the downhill traverse. The leafy trees framed the twilight sky. "Mother Nature did all the work. I was lucky enough to capture it." Her chest heaved, remembering the beauty of Alhambra and the hilltop city of Granada.

"How long will you be staying?" Greg asked.

"A few weeks at least. Get through the fair and make sure Aunt Lily is back on her feet, although her foot looks nearly healed already." She scanned the room. "Catch me up. Who are all these people? Do I know any of them?"

"Sam! How lovely to see you!" said Judith Whipley, president of the Women's Club, advisor to the Junior Women's Club and director of Modern Debutantes of Southern California.

Sam cracked a smile as Mrs. Whipley toddled toward them wearing a too-snug pencil skirt and her always present string of pearls. Her eyes scanned Sam up and down.

"Mrs. Whipley, it's so nice of you to come." Sam leaned in for a standard hug, but Mrs. Whipley opted for the two-cheek continental kiss.

"You must be so tired after your long journey. I prefer to rest and refresh after traveling before seeing anyone, but you young folks are so devil-may-care." She barely took a breath. "Ms. Quinlan, nice to see you away from Café Nate." She waved to someone across the room, said "Toodles," and dashed away.

Sam and Q looked at each other and giggled. "Whiplash Whipley hasn't changed a bit," Sam said.

"Nope. When she comes into the café, I just smile and nod and wait for the storm to pass."

"At least she acknowledged you. I'm clearly chopped liver," Greg said.

"Nothing wrong with chopped liver, baby," Q cooed. "Especially when it's a pate, spread on a slice of fresh baked French baguette and topped with caramelized onion."

"I'm realizing how hungry I am. I haven't eaten since the meal on the plane." Sam patted her stomach.

"We've got plenty of food. You mingle, and I'll fix you a plate." Q set off before Sam could protest.

"You'll have to mingle on your own. Joan just waved me over for something." Greg disappeared and Sam stood in the middle of the studio like an island in the stream when she heard some raised voices coming from the side. She recognized Mr. and Mrs. Carpenter, owners of the hardware store. They were in the middle of an animated discussion with someone whose back was to Sam and the gelled, shiny black hair didn't look familiar. Mr. Carpenter's arms made all kinds of movement in the air, and Mrs. Carpenter's finger was doing a lot of air poking.

"Eat up, my friend." Q presented a plate that actually had liver pate on it, along with cheeses, fruit, and petit fours.

Sam popped a liver pate and caramelized onion appetizer into her mouth. The savory creaminess of the pate with the mild sweetness of the onion and crusty French bread resulted in a very suggestive moan escaping from Sam.

Q giggled. "That sounded very much like a compliment."

Sam swallowed. "Most definitely. This is scrumptious. I could eat an entire sandwich of this."

Sam felt a small tug on her heart as she watched Q's face light up and a broad smile spread across her face. Even though they video chatted, called, and texted often, she hadn't realized how much she missed her friends and family, live and in person.

"Oh-mah-gawd, Sam! It's so good to see you."

Sam turned in the direction her elbow was pulled. It was the Patel twins, Mimi and Gigi. They were identical twins, but Gigi wanted Angelina Jolie's nose, so as soon as she turned eighteen, she got it from a doctor in Newport Beach. It definitely made it easier to tell them apart. Sam desperately tried to balance her plate as she once again found herself the filling in a sandwich hug.

"Wow, you guys, thank you so much for coming!" Sam said once they came out of the hug. "You both look stunning, as usual. How have you been?"

"Never mind us. We want to hear about your latest adventure," Mimi said.

But before Sam could answer, Aunt Lily swooped in. "Sorry to interrupt the reunion. Sam, you'll never guess who is here. Come with me."

"Let's have a catch-up at the café!" Sam called to the twins, who gave an enthusiastic thumbs-up.

Aunt Lily led Sam to a small group of people, none of whom she recognized.

"Sam, these ladies are in WB triple-OG with me," Aunt Lily said.

"WB—what?" Sam asked.

"Women Business Owners of Orange Grove. Sam, it is wonderful to meet you. I'm Edith," one woman said.

"And I'm Gertie. We were beginning to think you were a figment of Lily's imagination." The woman squeezed Sam's arm as proof that she was, in fact, real.

"Well, I knew she was real." An attractive woman in her fifties smiled at Sam.

Sam smiled. "I am most definitely real. I hope Aunt Lily hasn't bored you to death."

"You don't remember me, do you?" said the woman, much younger than the others.

Sam couldn't hide the blank look she knew she must have. "You do look familiar." Nothing came to mind as she chewed her bottom lip. "I'm so sorry. Please, remind me how we know each other."

"Abigail Reed. Well, Mrs. Reed to you."

The lightbulb went on. "Oh my God! Mrs. Reed! How are you? Are you still teaching? You look—"

Abigail laughed. "Fifty pounds lighter, and I got rid of the husband and the helmet hair."

Sam remembered the helmet style hair, now replaced with short, sassy spikes.

"You were one of my favorite teachers, even with the helmet hair."

"Abby's engaged now," Aunt Lily said.

"Congratulations! When's the big day?" Sam asked.

"Thanks, we haven't set a date yet. He's trying to get a new company off the ground." Abby craned her neck. "He's around here somewhere."

"Sam!" someone called from across the room.

"I guess I'd better mingle. It was so nice of you all to come. I would love to meet your fiancé, Mrs.—Ms. Reed."

***

Sam wanted a break from socializing and leaned against a wall in the corner, savoring a moment alone. A girl and her liver pate. She watched as Aunt Lily moved into the main area of the studio, the colorful billowing sleeves of her kaftan making her look like the social butterfly she was. Sam was a fly on the wall as she scanned and observed the party goers.

"Oh, there's Abigail with her new beau. I must say hello. Ciao for now." Mrs. Whipley's voice resounded from another group of party goers. Sam watched Mrs. Whipley as she darted from the group and her gaze followed her with the hope of catching a glimpse of the fiancé, but Whiplash's high bouffant hair style completely blocked him.

Sam heaved a sigh.

"Taking a break?" Greg asked as he and Q leaned back with her.

"After fourteen hours of flight and layover, I wasn't prepared for this. Thank you both so much. I appreciate—" Sam and everyone else turned towards the yelling that was taking place near the entrance.

Mrs. Whipley stepped back as another woman Sam hadn't previously noticed at the party screamed at Ms. Reed and the man, that she assumed, was her fiancé. Wearing a designer wrap dress and strappy heels with laces wrapped up to her calf, the younger woman looked to be around the same age as Sam. The fiancé moved between the two women as they swiped and snarled at each other.

Sam cocked her head to one side. "Q, did we go to high school with the younger one on the left?" she asked about the aggressor.

Q squinted.

"Put your glasses on," Greg said.

Q slid her glasses down from the top of her head. "Thanks, hon. Yeah, I think that's Leticia Pedroza. She's a big deal at some tech company in Irvine."

"Oh!" All three reacted when Abby Reed threw her drink in Leticia's face. Unlike in the movies, ice cubes flew out, hitting her face.

"You bitch!" Leticia screamed and flew past the man, lunging at Ms. Reed, both women toppling to the floor.

Sam overheard one of the WB-triple-OG ladies' comment on the unexpected floor show. "Good Lord, it's like *Dynasty*."

"Greg, will you help me with this?" Sam gave him a pleading look. She glanced around and didn't immediately see Aunt Lily, but knew her aunt wouldn't want any harm to come to anyone, let alone allow violence in her studio. Greg nodded, and they moved through the crowd with purpose. Before they could reach them, the man, who had been trying to pull the two women apart, got knocked over by a stray kick to the groin.

The entire party gasped.

Greg rushed over to him. "Can you stand?"

The man groaned and nodded. He stood bent over, and with Greg's help, shuffled off to the side.

Sam turned her attention to the entangled women. She was stern, but did not yell. "Ladies, please!"

The women continued to flail their arms at each other, some landing on the face and head, and others just catching the floor as they rolled and wobbled in a heap.

They really do look like cats in those videos. "Stop!" Sam grabbed for the nearest shoulder in an effort to pull them apart, but a brusque arm swing pushed her backwards. Another collective gasp. Sam stumbled, but did not fall.

Gritting her teeth, Leticia, straddled over Ms. Reed's bottom with one hand pressing on her back as the other hand waved a defiant finger, responded, "Not until she tells me what she's doing with my boyfriend."

Ms. Reed, who was quite fit, was able to turn her shoulder slightly and grab Leticia's free wrist. In the time it took to draw a breath, Ms. Reed flipped Leticia over, pinned her arms down, and fired back, "I'm not here with your boyfriend. I'm here with my fiancé!"

Chapter Two

"Your what?" Leticia spat the words. "You said you didn't believe in marriage!" Leticia glared at the man while struggling to wriggle out from under the older woman.

"That's enough!" Greg boomed and picked Ms. Reed off Leticia as if he was grabbing the Sunday paper off the front porch.

Sam rushed over to help Leticia to her feet. "Are you hurt, Leticia?" She gave her former classmate a once over to see if there were any obvious signs of physical damage.

"Oh, please, as if she could harm me." Leticia yanked her arm away and did a double take when she finally looked up and saw who had come to her aid. "You've got to be kidding me. Sam Gordon. When did you get back in town?" She brushed off her clothes. In high school, Leticia had been an interesting cross between mean girl and "it" girl. Seemed not much had changed.

"Just a couple of hours ago," Sam said.

"It's *her* welcome home party." Greg didn't temper his disdain.

Leticia didn't even attempt to hide her eye roll. "I hope you'll forgive this rude interruption to your welcome home party."

Sam wasn't sure how to respond to such a sarcastic apology and was saved when Aunt Lily suddenly appeared.

"Oh dear! Leticia, have some tea and let me look at you and make sure you're okay." Aunt Lily rushed to Leticia's side and waved Q, holding a tray with two cups of tea, over. Leticia's expression softened as she let out a heavy sigh. Even Leticia couldn't be rude to Aunt Lily.

"I'm fine, Aunt Lily. Really. I think I'd rather just leave." She squeezed Aunt Lily's hand and turned to exit when she spotted Ms. Reed, and her hackles went up like a flare.

Aunt Lily acted as if everything was normal and offered tea to Abigail, who stared warily at Leticia.

Greg still held Ms. Reed by the elbow when he said, "Maybe you three could take this outside." Sam spun around, but the fiancé was nowhere to be seen and Leticia stormed out.

Abigail exhaled as she accepted the cup from Aunt Lily. "I am so sorry. I hope this doesn't ruin the party."

Most of the guests were moving back into their conversational groups. Sam could only imagine what they were talking about.

"Nonsense! This will become a funny story you tell your grand-kids," Aunt Lily said.

"I'll probably kill him before I'll be able to laugh about it," Abigail said between sips.

Sam, Q and Greg barely had a minute to recover before Aunt Lily bustled over with a large serving tray filled with pastries that Q had brought from Café Nate. "Here, start passing these out so the guests can talk to you about all the scrumptious food and not the cat fight."

Q quickly took the tray from Aunt Lily. "I'll take it." Q nodded to Sam. "You go mingle."

"You can't tell me what to do," Sam teased.

"But I can, and I say, go mingle," Aunt Lily instructed in no uncertain terms.

Sam wandered over to the beverage table. She would need some liquid refreshment if she was going to be talking all night. Sam was deciding between mango green tea or pH-balanced water when a male behind her said, "I knew that guy was bad news."

"Excuse me?" Sam turned to see Eddie Carpenter Jr., the owner of Carpenter's Hardware, who had recently taken over for his dad.

"Junior! It's so great to see you."

"You're the star of the hour. Welcome back." Junior pulled her in for a tight squeeze.

"So, how do you know him? Did you know he was engaged to one and dating the other?" Sam asked, wondering what kind of trouble-maker he was, as if being a two-timer wasn't enough.

Disdain dripped as Junior spoke. "The guy's a full-blown con man. He came into the store with some cock and bull story about his funds being tied up internationally and could he get a line of credit since he had a lot of remodeling to do for his office. I said, 'Sure, fill out a credit application,' and handed him one. You know what he said?"

Sam shook her head listening intently, and he continued.

"He said he didn't have the documents that have his account num-bers. I said, 'No problem; you can fill it out online from home,' and I wrote the link address on the back of a business card."

Sam waited for more, then prodded him on. "And did he?"

Junior chortled. "No. He came back the next day and said his computer crashed. Can you believe this guy? He wanted to know if a gentleman's handshake would do until he got his computer fixed, but HE'S the tech guy so... wouldn't he have extras or certainly be able to fix it himself?"

"He might have needed parts," Sam mumbled to herself.

"Anyway, I told him I run my business by the book, so he was welcome to pay cash or use a credit card. Just as I expected, he left."

"That does sound––"

"Except, he came back when I wasn't around and spoke to my dad, who is a lot more old school."

"Oh, no." Sam winced in anticipation.

"Oh, yes. Dad gave him a twenty-thousand-dollar line of credit, and he's used every penny of it, and we haven't seen a dime."

I bet that's who the Carpenters were arguing with earlier. "I'm so sorry. Can you take legal action?" Sam asked.

"We've started the legal process, but it's slow. Besides, I'm a carpenter with a few tools in my belt to solve a problem. Sorry, Sam, I see someone I need to speak with." And with that, he dashed off.

Sam took the quiet moment to look around at all the people who had come to welcome her home. Q and Greg were still serving up food and making conversation. Aunt Lily laughed with Edith and Gertie, and as much as she enjoyed the party, Sam wished it was just the two of them, curled up on the sofa watching *Thin Man* movies and eating popcorn like they did when she was a teenager.

Chapter Three

"Joan, I'm going to wrap this up for you to take home," Aunt Lily said, stacking more than one foil-wrapped plate of food. Joan clucked her tongue in a half-hearted protest.

A chortle escaped Sam's lips. "Sorry. The futility of arguing with Aunt Lily and taking home leftovers just came screaming back to me."

Q, Greg and Joan joined in Sam's giggles.

"I've got some for you too, Q."

Q fired back quickly, "Oh no, you don't, Aunt Lily. I can get my food any time I want. Pack that up for you and Sam so you don't have to cook."

Greg was stacking the chairs when his phone chirped three times. "Babe, I gotta go. Can you get a ride home?"

"Now?" Q's pitch raised.

"You know how it is when a client is close to launch." He was by her side in three quick strides, kissing her forehead and cheek, and giving her soulful puppy dog eyes.

"Pfff! Like I could say no to those eyes." Q tilted her head and offered her cheek for another kiss.

"I'll take her. You go," Sam offered as he planted a kiss on Q's lips and dashed out the door.

Q sighed as she said, "At least he made it to the end of the party."

Sam strode next to her friend, putting an arm around her. "Now you can fill me in on the latest gossip."

Q laughed. "Greg has a better line on the 4-1-1 than I do, but I'm sure I've got a few updates for you."

"Are you ready to go, Aunt Lily?" Sam hollered toward the back room. Aunt Lily came out with an armful of canvases.

"Would you mind coming back for me after you drop off Q? I want to set up for tomorrow morning's class. That way we can have breakfast together."

"I don't want to leave you here alone," Sam said, knowing she was going to do as Aunt Lily asked.

"Joan's still here, and you'll be back in twenty minutes."

"Or less!" Q interjected. Sam punched her arm.

"Okay, I'll be right back. Lock the door behind me."

***

Sam snorted, trying to suppress laughter at seeing Q white knuckling it on the arm rest.

"I'm not driving that fast. You're just used to driving with Greg, who drives below the posted speed limit."

"And who stops at stop signs and doesn't think a yellow light means go faster," Q said matter-of-factly.

"I stopped," Sam whined.

Q raised her eyebrow and smirked, which only made Sam laugh.

"Okay, fine." As they rolled up to a stop sign, Sam said, "One-two-three. There." Her foot was back on the gas. "I counted to three."

Q rolled her eyes.

"Thank you so much for coming, and for the food." Sam decided to change the subject.

"It was our pleasure, hon! I'm just so happy to have you back." Q squeezed Sam's hand.

"I missed you guys so much," Sam said.

"And yet, you're always on your way somewhere else." Q's tone was more melancholic.

"Because I don't want you to get sick of me," Sam quipped back.

"As if."

Sam pulled up to the curb and affected her flight attendant voice. "We have arrived at your destination. You may undo your seat belts."

Q laughed, unhooking her seat belt and getting out of the car. She leaned in before closing the door. "Come to the café for lunch tomorrow."

"Done. I'll see you then." Sam watched Q walk up to the door, open it and wave back at her once she stepped inside the door. This was something they had started in high school. Sam waved as she pulled away.

She decided to take the long way back so she could drive through the Plaza circle, a roundabout instead of a traditional intersection which was one of the unique things about Orange Grove. In the very middle was a round island like a little park. This section of town was historic, and she loved seeing the brickwork and the façades of the shops and restaurants. She would have plenty of time to spend down here, so for now she didn't want to keep Aunt Lily waiting any longer.

***

Sam shook her head as she approached the wide-open door of All Souls Art & Craft Studio.

"Aunt Lily, you were supposed to lock the door behind me, not leave it open. Hey, what's with the lights?"

"AHHHHHHHHHH!!" A blood-curdling scream came from the back. Sam bolted through the dark studio.

"Aunt Lily! Where are you?" Sam shouted.

"Sam?" A quivery reply.

"Joan?"

"Over here."

Sam followed Joan's voice near the check-out counter, nearly tripping over things on the floor; she finally turned the flashlight from her phone on. She shined it on the floor to see where she was going. Broken glass and art supplies were all over.

"What happened? Where's—" Sam caught sight of Aunt Lily, lying on the floor, not moving. "Aunt Lily!" Sam rushed beside her and Joan, who had tripped over the body. Her gut lurched when she saw the blood pooling out Aunt Lily's forehead.

Phone already out, Sam dialed 9-1-1 on speaker. As it rang, she did a quick check on Joan, who had righted herself.

"Joan, are you okay? Are you injured?"

"I think so. I mean, I think I'm okay." Her voice warbled.

Afraid to move or turn Aunt Lily, Sam checked her pulse. She didn't have a mirror handy, so she slid her phone under Aunt Lily's nose to make sure she was still breathing. It fogged up.

"Joan, what happened?"

"I-I don't know. I was, uh, coming back from returning the centerpieces to May's and... it was dark——"

"Was the door wide open?" Sam interrupted.

"Yes, and I called out to your aunt when someone came barreling past me, nearly knocking me down."

"Someone else was in here?" Sam quickly raised her phone, still in flashlight mode, in a quick sweep around the dark store when she gasped, and Joan let out a squeak. There, not more than six feet away, was another body.

"Oh my god! Who is that?" Sam tried to hold the phone up higher to see better. "Joan, can you see who that is?"

Joan's eyes widened, her head made micro shakes back and forth and her breath quickened. Her entire being pleaded with Sam to not have to go near the body.

Sam kissed the back of Aunt Lily's hand. "Aunt Lily, I'm right here. I'm going to step over a few feet, and Joan is here too. We're going to make sure everything is okay." She passed Aunt Lily's hand over to Joan to hold.

Now that she knew it was a crime scene, Sam tried not to disturb all the items strewn on the floor as she got up to move closer to the other body. She slowly passed the phone light across the length of the body, like a light scan on a printer. She knew it was a man before she got to his face and then said, "He was at the party. It's Abigail Reed's fiancé!"

"What?" Joan's high pitch cracked, and she sounded as confused as Sam felt.

"9-1-1, what's your emergency?"

Sam shouted into the phone. "My name is Sam Gordon. I'm at—oh geez what's the street number—6745 Citron. All Souls Art and Craft Studio. My aunt is unconscious and bleeding. And I'm pretty sure a man has died. We need an ambulance."

"Have you checked if she's breathing?"

"Did you say he or she? She"—Sam emphasized the s-h— "is definitely breathing––"

"And she has a steady pulse," Joan said.

"And she has a steady pulse," Sam repeated to the 9-1-1 operator. "But the man" —she rested two fingers on his wrist—"isn't, I don't think. Breathing. I can't find a pulse and there's no chest movement."

"The ambulance should be there any minute. Is she on any medication?"

Sam said, "No."

Joan said, "Yes."

Sam looked at Joan.

"She's taking Lipitor for high cholesterol."

"Are you in any immediate danger?"

"No, ma'am. I don't think so." Sam's head darted around as if she was looking for a blind spot.

"Keep the line open, and I'll stay on until the officers arrive," the 9-1-1 operator instructed them.

Sam surveyed the scene. Still on the phone with the emergency operator, Sam swiped her phone to the camera icon. She started taking some photos and switched to video.

"For insurance," Sam whispered when she saw Joan watching her. She quickly panned as much of the room as she could before closing the camera. It would be dark and grainy, but it could be helpful.

Chapter Four

S am stared at the automated text message she had received from
Uncle Bill. *I'm soaring through the clouds right now. I'll get back
to you when I land.* She looked at Aunt Lily lying in the hospital bed.
The pit in her stomach grew as she tried not to remember her mother
in the hospital a lifetime ago.

Aunt Lily was healthy, even if she did look like a half-dressed mum-
my. She was wrapped in bandages that started just under her armpits
down to her waist, with a wrap around her head to top it off. It looked
like a pillbox hat. Sam smiled at the image as she squeezed Aunt Lily's
hand.

"I came as soon as I could. How is she? How are you? Was he really
dead?" Q rushed in with a stack of boxes from the café. "I've brought
Aunt Lily's favorite. Cheese with apricot Danish, quiche, fruit cups
and some very sinful hot caramel crunch lattes."

Q was non-stop motion as she spoke, setting up the hospital tray
table with all the goodies as though they were at a four-star restaurant.

Sam answered with the same quick cadence. "Aunt Lily's not awake
yet. The doctors said it could take a while for the sedative to wear off.
She's got a concussion, broken collar bone, a broken rib, and she broke
her leg that was almost healed, but other than that, she's fit as a fiddle.

I'm ... better now that you brought breakfast. Yes, very dead. Can you hook me up with a slice of quiche?"

"Do you know what happened?" Q asked as she handed Sam a slice of quiche adorned with fresh fruit and a Danish.

"No idea. Q, he was shot, and I know my aunt couldn't have done that." Sam leaned closer to Q, speaking a little more softly. She looked around, leaned in even closer.

"It was that guy. The one Ms. Reed and Leticia were fighting over."

"Wait. What?" Q's face screwed up in confusion. "Do you think one of the women came back looking for him and shot him?"

"It's a possibility, but the bigger question is why he came back to the studio after the party that he basically ran away from."

"Do I smell quiche?" Sam and Q snapped their heads toward Aunt Lily, whose eyes were slowly opening, and her throaty voice continued. "I don't suppose you brought cheese Danish?"

"Aunt Lily!" Sam squealed, then immediately dropped her volume.

"I'll grab the nurse." Q squeezed Aunt Lily's foot as she rushed out.

"It's so good to have you back!" Sam held Aunt Lily's hand in a double-fisted grip.

"Back? Where'd I go?" Aunt Lily's voice was still froggy. "Why can't I feel my hands?"

"What!" Sam looked down and realized she had a death grip on her aunt's hand, and she had probably cut off her circulation. Sheepishly, she let go. "Oh. Sorry."

"Dear, would you get me some water?" Aunt Lily asked, trying to clear her throat.

"I hear our patient is awake!" The doctor and a nurse strode in, with Q following.

The doctor came up alongside Sam as she whipped out her little pen light and started checking Aunt Lily's eye response time. The nurse came up on the other side of Sam, wanting to take Aunt Lily's pulse. Sam quickly stepped out of the way and stood next to Q at the foot of the bed.

The examination went on for a few minutes. "Okay, all the vitals look good. We are going to keep you overnight and see how you're doing tomorrow. Is there someone at home who will be able to assist, or do we need to arrange a recovery stay?

Sam raised her hand like she was in school. "I'll be there!"

"Great. We'll continue to check on you throughout the day and the nurse will go over how to keep the cast area watertight. Use the day to get lots of rest." Doctor and nurse exited as briskly as they had entered.

"That's great news! That calls for quiche and a cheese Danish." Q cheerfully prepared a plate for Aunt Lily.

Sam stepped to Aunt Lily's side again, grasping her hand. She exhaled a deep breath of relief, and felt her shoulders drop.

"Dear, I don't suppose I could have my hand back so I can eat Q's delicious breakfast?"

Sam looked at Q holding the plate out to them, then down at her resumed double-hand grip on her aunt's hand while her other was incapacitated.

"You mean your spirit guides can't feed you?" Sam teased as she let go, taking the plate from Q and setting it on Aunt Lily's lap.

"The spirits can do many things, but spoon feeding isn't one of them." Aunt Lily took a forkful of quiche into her mouth and made the universal sound for yumminess. "Q, this is delightful. Thank you so much."

Q beamed. "It's my pleasure. I'm so happy to see you up and eating before I go." She moved to the other side of the bed and kissed Aunt Lily on the cheek.

"Thank you, Q." She squeezed Q's hand.

"I'll check you later," Q said to Sam as she walked out.

Sam sat, watching Aunt Lily eat.

After several bites, Aunt Lily put her fork down and grabbed onto Sam's hand. "I'm so happy you're home."

"Me too."

"I'm okay. I'm not going anywhere."

"I know."

Sam could see Aunt Lily was studying her.

"I'll be home tomorrow, and I'll need you to get some things ready for me at home," Aunt Lily said in a very matter of fact tone.

"No problem. I'll get anything you need ready," Sam responded.

Aunt Lily took a breath. "Honey, I know how scary this is for you. I know that your parents said the same thing when your mom was so ill and in the hospital. This is different. I WILL be home tomorrow."

Sam could feel everything well up inside, but she would keep it there. "I know." Her warbly voice said otherwise.

"You can't stay here all day watching me eat and sleep. Have faith. I'll be home." Aunt Lily held up their clasped hands and gave a hard squeeze. "Okay?"

Sam could only nod as she bit her lip.

"Good. First thing we need to do is fix that ladder I tripped over so no one else gets hurt."

Sam's head snapped up. "What?"

"You're right. Let's just get a new one."

"Aunt Lily, don't you remember what happened?"

"Of course, I do. I fell off the ladder. I know, I know. I should've waited for you or Joan to come back, but that man, Abigail's fiancé, came in. Oh dear, I can't remember his name."

"He did? Why?" Sam tried not to sound too eager.

"I think he wanted to apologize, and I think he wanted to buy an apology gift for Abigail."

Sam's brow furrowed.

"You look just like your dad when you do that."

Sam widened her eyes to release the angry elevens between her brows.

"Did he say what he wanted to buy?" Sam asked.

"No. I think it was an afterthought once he started looking around the studio. He pointed to one of the paintings toward the ceiling." Aunt Lily's eyes focused upward as she recalled the memory.

"Which one was it?" Sam was drawing a blank as to what was hanging on the walls.

Sam could tell Aunt Lily was searching her memory as her eyes were searching. Sam touched her arm. "It's not important right now. You need to get some rest."

Sam leaned over and kissed Aunt Lily on the part of her forehead not wrapped in bandages, then made the grand announcement. "And I will leave you and get some things ready for tomorrow. But I will be back later."

Aunt Lily blew her a kiss as Sam walked out of the hospital room.

"Doctor!" Sam called out to the doctor standing at the nurse's station.

The doctor smiled as Sam approached. "Your aunt is doing very well."

"Is she? Because she doesn't seem to remember what happened. Well, she remembers some of it," Sam said, somewhat skeptical.

"That's natural. Things will be a bit fuzzy for her. She still has the anesthesia in her system, and her body has been through a trauma. Once she's more rested, everything will become clearer for her."

Everything the doctor was saying made sense. Sam knew she was probably worrying for no reason. There must be a logical explanation as to why a man came to apologize and buy a gift and ended up dead, with a bullet in his chest.

Chapter Five

S am barely made it to the kitchen counter before the paper grocery bags started to slip from her grip. She used her knee to stop the bags from sliding and hoisted them onto the counter secure and intact. She'd need to grab some of her aunt's reusable bags and stick them in the rental car.

Her mind wandered as she put away frozen pizza, frozen entrees, ice cream, a giant block of sharp cheddar and a jumbo bag of tortilla chips. Aunt Lily would never pollute her body with such things, which is why Sam had to go buy them.

A couple of quick knocks came on the door before it swung open and Greg stepped inside.

"You need to start locking this door."

"You wouldn't be able to pop in if we did," Sam quipped back.

Greg looked at the array of items still on the counter as he walked further in. "Don't let Q see this stuff."

"Don't tell her you saw it." Sam winked.

"You know she'd send over anything you wanted."

"Exactly! She doesn't need to constantly feed me and Aunt Lily."

Greg sat on a stool, leaning on the counter. "How are you doing?"

"They are going to release Aunt Lily tomorrow. Oh, so I think I need your help moving some things around." Sam continued to put away the last of the items.

"Absolutely, but I asked how YOU were doing." Greg looked at her pointedly.

Sam met his gaze, took a deep breath, and let it out. "Honestly, I'm not sure. I think I'll feel better once I know more about why he was in the shop. I mean, he was shot." Sam started to pace as she continued. "Did someone intend to rob the place, and he got in the way? What if he hadn't been there? Would they have shot Aunt Lily?" Sam's voice had become higher and choppy.

Greg hopped off the stool and held her by her arms. "Don't do that. Aunt Lily is fine." He pulled her in, hugging her.

Sam always liked Greg's hugs. She sighed. He was right. The 'what ifs' weren't good to dwell on, but the who, what and why whirled around her brain.

"Thanks," Sam said sincerely as she pulled, and then in her best boss tone, said, "Now, I need you to move the sofa along that wall and move the chair further into the corner and definitely push the coffee table back, so she has a nice open space to maneuver in."

"What will you be doing if I'm doing all the work?"

"Directing." Sam walked over the living room space. She loved the open floor plan, and it would be helpful when Aunt Lily came home. "Actually, I'll be clearing some space before you move the sofa."

Aunt Lily had beautiful baskets filled with yarn in various stages along the wall Sam wanted the sofa moved to. It looked like each basket represented a different project. There were a few that were knitting or crochet, but this last one looked like a sewing project.

Sam and Greg stepped back and admired their handiwork as a voice came from behind them.

"Ha! How did I know you'd be here?" Q stood with her hands on her hips as she surprised them with a mocking tone and a big smile.

Greg laughed as he walked over to Q, kissing her and putting his arm around her waist. "Because you knew I'd want to check on her. And I'm pretty sure I told you."

Q shrugged. "That's true. I thought I'd bring some eats by for you, Sam."

Sam and Greg looked at each other and laughed.

"What?" Q asked innocently.

"Nothing. I am hungry, though. What did you bring?" Sam looked at the insulated bag sitting on the kitchen counter, realizing they hadn't even heard her come in and set it down.

"Kale, cranberry and walnut salad and lemon meringue for dessert," Q announced as she pulled out containers from the bag. "Guess who came into the café today? I'll just tell you. Leticia!"

Sam spun around from the silverware drawer. "Really?" Sam asked excitedly.

"Yeah, and I don't think she knows that guy is, you know—"

"Dead," Greg finished her sentence.

"That's possible." Sam mused, "I doubt the police have notified anyone at this point. Do police notify girlfriends and fiancés?" They both looked at Greg.

Not waiting for an answer, Q started. "I think the police will definitely want to interrogate Leticia."

"Why?" Sam's eyes were wide with expectation.

"She said, and I quote, *He'll pay for humiliating me like that!*" Q said with dramatic flair.

"Why did she say that? I mean, that seems random," Sam continued to probe.

"She sat at the counter, and I was pouring her coffee when she blurted that out," Q explained.

"Sounds like a guilty conscience," Sam stated.

"Sounds like you girls need to stop speculating and let the police handle it," Greg interjected.

Sam rolled her eyes, and Q raised a brow.

Greg sighed. "I'm going to work." He looked pointedly at Q. "You should do the same. And you..." He turned toward Sam. "Finish getting ready for Aunt Lily, and let me know if you need help with any more heavy lifting."

"You know she can move the furniture on her own," Q quipped.

"I know. I'm just glad she pretends to need help. It means there's hope for her yet." He winked.

"What's that supposed to mean?" Q asked.

Sam laughed and started to explain. "You've heard of 'opening the pickle jar'?"

"Yeah...even though you can open the pickle jar, you ask him to do it so he feels needed or something like that?" Q summarized the theory with a confused look on her face.

"Greg, your hopeless romantic boyfriend, thinks that since I'm willing to ask him to move furniture, even though I could do it myself, I am open to asking someone to open the pickle jar for me," Sam concluded.

Greg beamed. Q shook her head and kissed him.

"Thank goodness you're my romantic weirdo."

"That's a win! And now I take my leave." Greg raised his arm in victory as he walked out the door.

***

A shower and a change of clothes was exactly what Sam needed after spending the night in the hospital and getting things ready for Aunt Lily to come home tomorrow. Sam unpacked her suitcase like an automaton, deep in thought about the events of the last twenty-four hours. Definitely not the homecoming she had expected.

Sam shoved her empty suitcase into the closet and looked around the room. Everything looked the same. The room revealed a little timeline into Sam's young life. The bookshelves started with Encyclopedia Brown, Nancy Drew, John Grisham, and Patricia Cornwell. A stuffed Scooby-Doo shared the bed with a giant teddy bear and a rainbow-sequin pillow. The walls had posters of boy bands and celebrity crushes, and a prized, vintage concert poster for Bob Dylan featuring Led Zeppelin, Eric Clapton, and Jimi Hendrix. She had inherited it from her dad, who used to always tell her, "This is real music, not those girly boy bands."

The bed creaked and sagged when she plopped onto It. "Yikes, I think It's time for a new mattress." Propping herself up on the bed, she pulled out her phone and opened up the pictures. The screen looked black since it defaulted to the last picture, or video, in this case. Sam touched the play button.

It was dark to start, but once she turned on her phone light, she could see what the camera was pointing at. Joan, pale and shaken. The image panned out to try to capture some of the damage. It became grainy as the light strained to reach the depths into the studio, then as the camera panned further, the picture wobbled as Sam saw the other body and she could hear herself and Joan gasp. Sam froze the video once it had a solid capture of the man. It was definitely the man Leticia and Abigail were fighting over.

Why did he really come back?

Sam zoomed into the picture. There was a tattoo peeking out from his sleeve, around his bicep. She rotated it to get a better angle, then zoomed in as far as it would go.

"That looks like—" Sam took her free hand up to her neck, grasped the gold chain and pulled out the necklace tucked into her shirt. She held it out, next to her phone.

"Ruh-Roh."

Chapter Six

Sam's brain was in overload. *Do I know him? He didn't look familiar. Maybe he was one of Dad's friends? Could he have been looking for me or...just sheer coincidence?*

"I'm going to drive myself crazy!" Sam shouted to the empty room.

Her phone rang and the caller ID said OGPD. She answered quickly. "Sam Gordon."

There was a pause. Sam smirked. This happened all the time. People were expecting a male voice when they had the name Sam Gordon.

"Uh, hi, I'm trying to reach Sam Gordon."

"You've reached her."

"Right. I'm Detective Jack Finn. I'd like to get your statement of events from last night."

It was more of a statement than a question, but Sam jumped on the opportunity.

"Absolutely. I'll be there in fifteen minutes."

"Ma'am, you don't have—"

"Oops!" Sam looked at the phone that she'd just hung up, cutting off the detective. "Sorry!"

Sam grabbed her notes, her bag, and her phone and dashed out of the room, rushed down the hall, snatched the key fob off the kitchen counter and sailed out the door.

She buckled up and immediately pressed the call button on her steering wheel. "Call Q mobile." It was answered on the second ring.

"Hey, can't chat for long. Large crowd just came in. How is Aunt Lily?"

Sam shouted to be heard over the sounds of clanging of pots and pans, and a blender whirring coming through the speakers. "She's resting. I'm on my way to the station to give my statement."

"Oh?" Q sounded skeptical.

"You think it's okay if I ask questions too?"

"It's called a STATEMENT for a reason," Q said.

"I know, but—"

"Sam, let them ask the questions. You'll be surprised how much you can learn just by listening to what they're asking."

"Good point. I knew I liked you," Sam said.

"I gotta go. Behave yourself!"

"You're not the boss of me." Sam giggled and ended the call.

The last time Sam had visited the Orange Grove Police Station was during a high school civics class field trip. The station had undergone a remodel to Craftsman architecture instead of the lackluster commercial look that seemed to be popular in the sixties. She walked up the steps and was pleasantly surprised by the exposed beams under the wide, overhanging eaves. Upon entering, the interior had been upgraded as well and the walls were painted in soothing blues.

"Gosh, I don't even feel like I'm in a police station," Sam mumbled to herself.

"Have you been in many?" A low southern drawl came from an officer standing behind the large U-shaped reception area. He reminded Sam of a giraffe with the head of a golden retriever. His lopsided smile let her know he was teasing.

"Oddly enough, I have. But only as a visitor." Sam winked.

He opened his mouth then stopped, held one finger up, the universal sign for *one moment*, and tapped his headset.

Sam wandered over to a wall lined with pictures of the officers in the community. "Oh, they still do Treats in the Streets at Halloween!" Sam exclaimed as she remembered dressing up in her costumes and going to Old Town where the streets were blocked off and the shops and restaurants gave out candy to the kids. It seemed to have been quiet for a minute or two, so Sam moseyed back to the reception desk.

"I'm here for Detective"—she peeked at a scrap piece of paper tucked in her jean pocket— "Jack Finn."

He held his finger up again and mouthed *sorry* to her. Sam gave him a thumb's-up. She waited as he nodded in response to the person on the other end of the call. His lips parted as if to speak, then closed again. Sam read his name badge. Officer Riley Decker was certainly getting an earful. "I've made notes and will make sure to relay your concerns and suggestions to the Chief, Mrs. Whipley."

Sam let out a guffaw and slapped her hand over her mouth.

His eyes crinkled as he smiled. "Thank you, ma'am, I surely will." He tapped his headset ending the call. "I take it you are familiar with Mrs. Whipley?"

"Yes, sir, I am indeed."

"Thank you so much for your patience. I think you said you're here to see Detective Finn?" He tapped a few keys on the computer.

"Yes. I'm here to give my statement regarding an incident at my aunt's studio."

"Samantha Gordon?"

"Yes. Please just call me Sam."

"Miss Gordon, please have a seat. I'll let him know you're here." His outstretched arm indicated the rows of chairs off to the side.

She took a seat and pulled out her phone and checked social media to see if anything was going on she wouldn't want to miss out on. Kittens and puppies were still adorable, and she had nine friend requests from some very clever trolls. "Delete. Delete. Delete." She sighed heavily. "Why don't you use your powers for good?" she scolded her phone.

"I don't think they can hear you." Officer Decker stood in front of her.

She laughed and craned to look up at him. *Geez, he really was a giraffe.*

"It'll be a short wait. The detective is finishing up another interview. Can I offer you some coffee?"

"You may." Sam watched the officer go around a corner, and she could hear a whirring sound.

Moments later, he held out a blue ceramic mug with OGPD on one side and a gold shield on the other. It smelled of caramel and was frothy on top.

"Wow, you must have one of those super fancy coffee-espresso machines back there." She took the mug and inhaled.

"It's not exactly New Orleans style café ole, but I've become creative with the coffee dispenser. Hope you like it."

Sam blew into the cup, gently breaking the frothy surface, and took a sip. Her eyebrows shot up. "This is delicious! I can't believe you made this from a coffee dispenser."

Officer Decker smiled and walked back behind the desk. "The coffee's not bad, but it's nice to have a little reminder of home."

"You're from New Orleans, then?" Sam sipped carefully.

"Family's originally from Nawlins. I came here by way of Houston."

"Really? How long have you been in Orange Grove?"

"Nine months this weekend." Officer Decker turned his attention to a young boy followed by a woman Sam presumed to be his mother. "How can I help you?"

Sam busied herself reading an email she received from one of the twins she'd nannied for at her last job. "Sam, can't you please come back? The new nanny is an absolute nutter!" She tried not to spew coffee when she guffawed. She rushed to the desk and Officer Decker plucked two tissues and held them out for her.

"Y'all have a nice day," he said as the mother and son left. "Do you need a paper towel or anything, Miss Gordon?"

Sam blotted around her mouth and down the front of her shirt. "I think I got it. Just a few droplets."

"Officer Decker." A male voice came from behind the officer. "I'm ready for Miss Gordon."

"Detective Finn, she's right here."

Sam peered around to see a very buttoned-down gentleman in a midnight blue three-piece vested suit and black shoes that looked like her Uncle's Florsheim's. As she made her way around the desk, her flip flops caught the corner of the carpet runner, and her feet became entangled, and she stumbled forward. "That was a close call." Sam quickly offered her hand to shake and hoped the flush of embarrassment she felt didn't show on her face. "I'm Sam Gordon. It's a pleasure—it's not a pleasure, I mean, hi, nice to meet you."

His arms were already outstretched in preparation for the crash that had been coming. He nodded, shaking her hand.

"Yes. Please follow me." He turned and started walking.

Sam looked at Riley, who nodded for her to follow him. She trotted to catch up with him, following him through a set of double doors. Now it looked like a police station. Little islands of desks faced each other. She followed him to one, where he motioned for her to sit in the chair beside it.

"Thank you for coming in. For the record, I'm Detective Jack Finn."

Wow, this guy is all business, Sam thought as she watched him neatly drape his jacket on the back of his chair, take his seat and pull a tiny recorder from his pocket and set it on the desk.

"I like to record in case I miss something while I'm taking notes."

"Sure."

"I know some of this will seem repetitive, but I still have to ask. What time did you arrive at the studio?" the detective began.

"10:01," Sam stated matter of fact.

"That's oddly specific."

"I was exhausted and doing that time calculation thing when you travel from another time zone. You know. You look at the time and calculate, *it's really six AM.*"

"So, you came from the UK?"

Oy, he's a bright one! The voice in Sam's head had a cockney accent, and she bit the inside of her lip to stop herself from laughing out loud.

The detective scribbled in his notepad and stopped when the table shimmied.

"Sorry. My leg hit the leg of the table." She grimaced.

"Mm-hmm, and what did you see when you entered?" he asked, scribbling in his notepad.

"Uh, well, nothing at first. It was—"

"And why was that?" the detective asked without looking up.

"The lights were off. It wasn't until—"

"Is that normal?" he interrupted again, without looking at her.

"Well, yes. We had just had a party—" Sam started.

"What kind of party?" Detective Finn interrupted.

"A surprise party. For me. Although I'm the one who surprised them." Sam started to giggle when she saw the detective's blank expression and went back to the facts.

"Yes, and she was setting up for the morning art class—Oh crap! Sorry, I just realized no one canceled the class, but I guess they probably figured it out when they saw the crime scene tape this morning. Anyway, that's why it was odd that it was dark when I pulled up."

Detective Finn nodded slowly as he scribbled. Sam fidgeted until she just couldn't wait any longer.

"Do you know who that man was? He was at the party, but he left. Why did he come back? What did he want with my aunt?" Sam took a breath.

Detective Finn maintained direct eye contact and calmly answered her questions in succession.

"We're waiting for confirmation on his identity. His wallet was missing. We don't know why he came back. It may not have anything to do with your aunt, but we will find out." Detective Finn's voice was warm and sincere, but patience wasn't one of Sam's strengths.

Detective Finn continued with his questions. "You mentioned he left the party."

"He came with Abigail Reed, and I honestly didn't notice him until Leticia Pedroza came in and, oh man, did the claws come out!"

Detective Finn raised a brow for her to continue.

"Apparently, he was seeing both of them, but he was supposedly engaged to Abigail and leading Leticia on. I think she saw them through the window and came in, fists flying. Well, the drinks went flying." Her animated tone brought a curl to the corner of the detective's mouth.

"And what was he doing during all this?"

"I think he was as shocked as the rest of us at first, but by the time it broke up, he was gone." Sam watched his pen swirl and sway as he scribbled away.

"So, you came back. It was dark; then what?" the detective started again.

Sam nodded, remembering where they left off.

"The door was wide open. I'd told her to lock it when I left so I started to tease her about it as I entered, and that's when I heard the scream." She shuddered.

"And what did you see?"

"Right, umm, well, I rushed toward the scream, and I saw her lying on the floor. I didn't see Joan until I came around the table. She was kneeling next to my aunt." Sam felt her blood pulsing faster as she recalled how she had found her aunt.

Detective Finn must have heard it in her voice. "You're doing fine. I'm sure it was quite a shock to see her like that."

Sam let out the breath she didn't know she was holding.

Detective Finn flipped through his notes before he started again.

"I listened to the 9-1-1 call, and it sounds like that was when you saw the other body."

"Yeah, I turned on my phone light to see if I could see what she tripped on or fell on and I saw him."

"Did you notice anything?"

"I noticed all the blood on his chest." That came out a lot more sarcastic than Sam intended. "I mean, there was a lot of it. You couldn't not see it."

"Was he alive when you saw him?"

"Oh God, no! I'm sorry. I don't mean to sound so callous."

Detective Finn tried to reassure her. "You don't sound callous."

Sam smiled, and Detective Finn's brows raised when she told him that she checked for a pulse and put her phone under his nose to check for breath on the screen. She wasn't sure what that meant.

Detective Finn thanked her for her patience and announced, "Just a couple more questions. Could you tell if anything was missing?"

"No. It was dark at first and then everything was so chaotic once the police and ambulance arrived. Plus, I've been away so I probably wouldn't know if something was missing." And then she added, more to herself, "I guess I'll have Joan help me with that."

"Final question. Do you have any reason to believe Miss Harris had anything to do with what happened?"

"Joan? Are you serious? No!" Sam emphasized this with crossed arms.

"I have to—"

"I mean, seriously. You can't be serious!" Sam stood abruptly.

"It's standard—"

Sam cut the detective off again, arms moving to illustrate every word. "Have you met Joan? She doesn't just move a spider outside. She moves their web as well!"

Detective Finn put his hand up in stop motion. "Miss Gordon, I'm not accusing her of anything. It's a standard question. I'll ask her the same of you when I get her statement."

Chapter Seven

S am gave Detective Finn all the details. Except one.

She was still getting the automated text reply from Uncle Bill. He must have been home by now. She might wake him, but she needed to see him.

Uncle Bill wasn't a blood uncle. He had met her parents in college back east, and they became fast friends. He and her dad had both joined the service. After Uncle Bill left the Army, he moved to Orange Grove to put his journalism degree to work at the County Herald. Her parents fell in love with the town when they visited their friend and moved here too. He had become co-guardian of her when her dad died, alongside Aunt Lily.

The porch light was on when Sam pulled into the driveway. *That's a good sign.*

She pulled a key out immediately after she rang the bell. *I could just use my key. But he may be sleeping or tired and not want any company. You could just peek in and—*

Her mental sparring match ended when a bear of man, with a grizzly beard to match, swung the door open, scooping her up before she knew what was happening. Her whole being felt safe, loved and almost out of air.

"You're smothering me, Uncle Bill!"

"Kiddo! You're a sight for sore eyes." His voice boomed in her ear.

He plopped her back onto her feet and held her out in front of him. "Let me look at you. Have you grown?" He started squeezing her biceps, and Sam giggled.

"Uncle Bill. I'm the same height as I was the last time you saw me."

"You've got some muscle on you." His eyes sparkled as he teased her.

"Uncle Bill!" Sam was chastising him now. She noticed his worn duffel on the floor, and he was wearing his sheepskin jacket.

"Did you just get in?"

"Just now. I pulled into the garage minutes before you pulled into the driveway."

"I'm so glad you're home. You're never going to believe what's happened."

"I want to hear all about it, but could it wait until I wash three continents worth of travel grime off me?" His forehead wrinkled and he raised his eyebrows in his plea to be refreshed.

Aunt Lily is safe in the hospital; what's a few more minutes? "Of course. I'll make us something to eat and some tea," Sam said.

"I don't know what you'll find in the way of food, but whatever you make will be great. Give me twenty minutes." Bill gave her another hug. "It's so great to have you home."

"Right back at ya," Sam replied.

Sam did a quick check in his kitchen. Nothing in the fridge except a fuzzy block that Sam guessed used to be cheese. Lots of condiment packages from fast food restaurants. In the cupboards, there was pasta but no sauce, not even canned tomatoes. She pulled her phone out and texted, *Food 9-1-1—Need Chicken Alfredo with broccoli, garlic bread and house salad, Uncle Bill's. Please & thank you!*

Fifteen minutes later, a delivery driver from Café Nate was at the door with a tote bag that smelled delicious.

After Sam set the bag on the counter to unpack the food, she found two slices of cheesecake perched on top. She quickly texted Q. *Thanks, girl! You're the best.*

She plated the food when she heard Uncle Bill's not so soft patter come down the stairs.

"You were right. There wasn't enough of anything to combine into a meal, or even a snack so ... ta-dah!" She timed it perfectly with the tea pot whistle.

Uncle Bill whisked the tea pot off the burner and set it aside as he inhaled the aroma of roasted garlic. "Mmm, good call. Earl Grey or ... white hibiscus something?"

"Someone is in the Tea Blend of the Month club," Sam teased.

"Even if I wasn't, your aunt would still send them to me," Bill reasoned.

"That's for sure. She sent me care packages with all her different blends every few months."

Bill slid onto the stool at the high kitchen counter, while Sam climbed up it.

"Uncle Bill, have you listened to your voice mails?"

"Oh, thanks for reminding me. I need to turn it back on." He reached into his back pocket and came up empty.

"I must've left it upstairs. Remind me when we're done eating."

Sam just shook her head. She didn't know whether to chastise him or praise him for not being glued to his phone.

"What am I going to do with you?"

"Well, I'm here now. You can tell me in person." He had an egg-sized swirl of fettuccine on his fork that went eagerly into his mouth as Sam began.

"I guess the short story is, Aunt Lily's in the hospital because of a dead man in the studio."

Bill choked, trying not to spit out the pasta he'd just put in his mouth. "What? Give me the long story."

"Sorry, I thought I'd rip off the Band-Aid. I guess I should have waited until you were done with that."

Uncle Bill raised one eyebrow and lowered his head ever so slightly. How many times had Sam received this silent but loud indicator that she needed to get to the point?

"Right, so Aunt Lily had a surprise welcome home party for me, and this man came as the date of one of my high school teachers. Well, then this other woman came too—you remember Leticia Pedroza—anyway, after they fought, he was gone but must've come back after the party looking for something, and when I came back to pick her up, the lights were off and I heard a scream and that's when I found her and the man from earlier, only he was dead." Sam exhaled.

Bill nodded. "What happened to Lily?" he asked calmly.

"She thinks she fell off a ladder. She has a broken collar bone, two fractured ribs, a broken leg, and they had to reset the foot that was almost healed. Oh, and a concussion. Which is why they are going to keep her until tomorrow. She's resting now."

"She *thinks* she fell off a ladder?"

"I'm not sure she remembers the man; at least, she didn't this morning. I didn't say anything about him. The doctor said she will likely remember everything later today or tomorrow. Trauma to the system and drugs in her system."

"How did he die? Sam?" Bill asked again when Sam didn't answer right away.

"Single gunshot to the chest." Sam watched as he took a slow breath. "Aunt Lily doesn't even own a gun, let alone know how to shoot one," she added.

"And there was no one else there?" he asked.

"Joan got there just before me. That's whose scream I heard. Joan said there was someone else, but it was dark and she never saw them."

"Then how does she know they were there?"

"They bumped into her as they were running out."

"So, a robbery gone wrong then."

Sam wasn't sure if he was asking a question or making a statement.

Sam confirmed his assumption. "That's how the police seem to be leaning."

Uncle Bill popped the last bite of his garlic bread into his mouth, put his silverware on his completely empty plate, and stood to move it to the sink. "But you don't think that's what happened."

She craned her neck to look at him from her seated position and silently shook her head.

He moved deliberately from the sink to the refrigerator. She could see the wheels turning. He came back with bottled water for both of them.

"You know what I'm going to say."

"I will let the police handle it, but I want to look into a few things too." Sam might as well be sixteen again, trying to convince him to let her go to a party by telling him how responsible she would be.

She didn't wither under his stare. Something she'd also learned not to do by the time she was sixteen.

His sigh of resignation as he sat back down let her know she'd won. Although Sam wasn't sure this was a winning situation.

"Tell me what you're looking into."

Sam grabbed her phone and performed finger acrobatics of a swipe, touch, and a pinch-and-spread before she flipped it around to show him a picture of the man's face that she found from the party. She knew Uncle Bill could handle seeing the other not-so-alive picture, but this was a better one for identification purposes.

"Is this the guy?" he asked as he took the phone from her with squinty eyes.

"Yes. Does he look familiar to you at all?"

"Familiar to me?" He pulled out his glasses and put them on, manipulating the size of the picture to get a better look. "Not really. Should he?"

Sam grabbed the phone, fingers dancing on the screen then flipped it back to him. "Look familiar?"

He stared at the phone, taking it for a closer look, then looked at Sam's neckline. "What do the police think?"

Sam chewed on her bottom lip.

"Sam?"

"You always told me a good investigator will hold back a piece of evidence."

"Yes, for an investigative report or detective, which you are neither." His tone was becoming sterner by the word.

"Uncle Bill," Sam pleaded.

Bill leaned back, studying her as if he was looking at charts and graphs.

Sam interrupted his thought process. "If it helps, they didn't say anything about it either so, you know...if we're both holding on to the same information, it's like it doesn't exist." Sam sat taller with a sly grin.

"Kid, this isn't the same as finding out who stole the cash register from the cafeteria."

"I know, and I'll be careful and discreet. I promise."

"You will and you'll keep me in the loop. At all times."

"At all times," she repeated and held up her right pinky.

As he wrapped his sausage-sized pinky around hers, he added, "And if you don't, I'll call the police."

"Hey!"

"Too late, we pinky swore."

Sam couldn't believe he just used her old trick on her. That was how she would throw in a later curfew or get the car for the night. The pinky swear was their bond.

"Okay, fine then, since you're the first person I'll be interviewing." Sam looked at her watch. "You're getting a reprieve since I've got to go back home before I head back to the hospital. I forgot to grab Aunt Lily's things before I went down to give my statement."

Uncle Bill gave her one of his lopsided smiles that was a blend of placating, acceptance, and love. He wrapped her in his arms, kissing the top of her head. "I'll see you at the hospital then."

Sam, strapping in her seatbelt, said to her empty car, "I don't know if I'm excited or scared." She checked her rear view mirror and backed out of the driveway.

Chapter Eight

Sam approached the hospital room with a hand-printed canvas tote bag that one of Aunt Lily's patrons had made for her. It had sweeping vines with bright flowers accented throughout. Sam didn't consider herself a floral person, but she always really liked this bag. She spied Uncle Bill and Aunt Lily holding hands over the bed railing. Growing up, she thought they might get together, like on one of those romantic comedies, but they never did. They raised her together, living separately. And why not? They'd inherited her, so it wasn't like they were a couple to start with. They were great friends and allies, though, and Sam couldn't have wished for two better people, other than her actual parents, to parent and mentor her. Aunt Lily was definitely the fun one, while Uncle Bill was the disciplinarian. It was very much like her friends who had divorced parents.

"Get a room!" she teased as she entered. "Oh wait, this is one."

"Bill was just catching me up on his adventures," Aunt Lily said.

"And your Aunt Lily was just catching me up on your adventures," Bill said, still holding Aunt Lily's hand.

Sam feigned shock.

"Whatever could you be referring to?"

"You neglected to tell me about getting lost in the Black Forest or discovering a century-old skeleton."

"Clearly, I didn't get lost, or I wouldn't be here." Sam flashed a wide grin. She set the bag at the foot of the bed. "I added some goodies that Q sent over." Sam patted the bag.

"Lily was telling me what happened last night," Bill said in a tone that intrigued Sam.

"Everything was so fuzzy this morning. Anyway, I was just telling Bill about that gentleman, and I use the term loosely, that Abigail brought to the party." Her brows furrowed. "Donny or Toby. It's on the tip of my tongue."

"That was quite a cat fight." Sam pulled napkin wrapped dinner-ware from the bag.

"It was indeed. Both those girls deserve better. You know poor Leticia has such a hard time finding a good man who's not intimidated by an executive woman—"

Bill interrupted what was sure to be one of Aunt Lily's tangents. "Tell Sam about the gentleman coming back to the store."

Sam was pretty sure her own tangential ability was inherited from her, if something like that could be inherited. She prompted with, "Really?"

"Yes, I'd just sent Joan to return the vases we borrowed to May Flowers when he came in. He said he wanted to apologize for disrupting the party."

"That was nice of him," Sam commented, hoping there was more.

Lily continued, "I thought so too, and then he started asking about the studio."

"Did it seem like he was casing out the studio?" Uncle Bill asked.

"Casing? Psh, no. I think he just felt bad about the party and wanted to make some polite small talk."

"And then what?" Sam asked, knowing there was more, but wondering if Aunt Lily remembered it.

"He saw that I had my hands full with easels and canvases, so he helped me set up and, oh! He asked about one of the pieces on the wall."

Sam and Bill looked at her, waiting.

"It was one of the surfing lithographs from that photographer you like," Aunt Lily added.

Sam knew it well. It was one of her favorite pictures that hung in the studio. It was like being in the middle of a sparkling green and turquoise glass tube. It was technically for sale, but Aunt Lily hung it high to discourage potential buyers. Her logic was that only a serious buyer would ask her to bring it down.

"And he wanted to buy it?" Bill asked.

"That's what I thought at first. I'd told him the price, and he said he was looking for something exactly like that for his office. I brought out the ladder and he offered to go up, and I told him I couldn't let him due to liability--"

"You went up the ladder with your foot in a cast?" Sam interjected in a pitch higher than she intended.

Aunt Lily simply continued. "But when I got up there, he asked about the one next to it."

Sam searched her memory for what was next to it. To the left was a tapestry, and on the other side... Sam's eyes widened, and she stifled a gasp, trying to sound nonchalant.

"The photo collage?" Sam asked.

"Yes. I told him it wasn't for sale and pointed out the sign on the frame. He said he understood and asked who created it. I didn't want to stay up there any longer than necessary, so I asked him if he still wanted the lithograph. He said he did, so I reached up to remove it from the wall and next thing I know, I'm waking up here."

"Do you think he caused you to fall?" Bill asked.

"Heavens, no! I probably just lost my footing when I reached up," Aunt Lily replied.

"Do you remember hearing anything while your back was to the store? Any other voices?" Sam pressed.

Aunt Lily looked up as though the answer was on the ceiling.

"Yes, someone else must have come in because I thought he was talking to me, but I couldn't hear him and then ... there was a bump on the ladder." She said each word slowly as the memory returned to her. "I remember trying to grab the top of the ladder for balance, but the whole ladder must've come down." Aunt Lily shuddered a little when she finished.

Uncle Bill, still holding Aunt Lily's hand, gave it a squeeze, and Sam grabbed her other hand.

"I'm going to be all right. No need to worry." Aunt Lily raised both of her clasped hands, then added, "I'm sure if you talk to ... Tony, I think his name was, he'll be able to fill in the blanks."

Sam gave Uncle Bill a look.

"I'm sure that's exactly what the police are doing," Sam reassured her.

Aunt Lily smiled and nodded. She looked tired. Sam shouldn't have pressed so much. She unzipped the tote.

"Are you ready for a creamy, rich slice of New York cheesecake?" Sam produced a pie slice-shaped container, a fork and several cups of various toppings.

"Q didn't know what you'd be in the mood for, so you have your choice of dark chocolate cherry, white chocolate raspberry, caramel apple, or ... strawberry," Sam finished the choices.

Sam smacked Uncle Bill's hand as he tried to dip a finger into the dark chocolate cherry. Aunt Lily chose strawberry. Uncle Bill kissed Aunt Lily on the cheek before announcing he was going to go.

"Jet lag is starting to set in, so I'm going to leave you, but call me as soon as the doctor gives the release order and I'll be here lickity split."

"I'll pick her up, Uncle Bill."

"How do you suppose you will lay her down comfortably in your little car?"

Sam gave Aunt Lily a once over. She was basically in a body cast. "Right. Okay then, you'll take her home, and I'll be there waiting."

Uncle Bill did the 'you got it' point and made a clucking sound. Sam turned back to Aunt Lily. "I brought a book that has crosswords, word jumbles and sudoku, or we have Trivial Pursuit or—"

"Honey, I think I just want to sleep. You don't mind, do you?"

"Of course not. You go ahead. I'll just sit over here and pick a crossword that will make me feel smart." Sam started to flip through the book as she took the chair near the window.

"Don't be silly. You go on home. It's going to be dark soon, and I'm likely to fall asleep soon anyway."

"Are you sure?"

"Yes, dear. Go visit Q and Greg. You must have a million things to catch up."

You have no idea, Sam thought.

Chapter Nine

S am stepped into the hall from Aunt Lily's hospital room when she nearly tripped over Joan, who sat on the floor against the wall, hugging her knees.

"Joan?" Sam was surprised to see her. Joan didn't respond, so she knelt beside her.

"Joan, are you okay? Aunt Lily is going to be fine." Sam put her hand on Joan's shaking shoulders. "Go in and see for yourself."

Joan finally looked up, her face wet with tears.

"I can't. Seeing her like that. Oh, Sam! I'm so sorry," she cried.

"Don't be silly. None of this is your fault. I'm the one who's sorry. I shouldn't have left until we were all ready to leave together." Sam squeezed Joan's arm.

"No. You don't understand." Joan waved her hand with a wadded-up tissue that disintegrated with each movement. She produced another crumpled tissue from inside her pocket. Sam waited as Joan blew her nose and composed herself. She sucked in a few quick breaths, pushing back the tears. Sam saw how distraught Joan was, but when she tried to speak, Joan held her hand up. "No, I need to tell you this. It's just... I'm so ashamed." Joan's head dropped.

"Joan, you can tell me anything. You're one of Aunt Lily's dearest and trusted friends. Whatever you have to say, you won't get any judgment from me."

Sam's words had the opposite effect she'd hoped for. Joan's eyes welled up with tears again. Sam handed her a fresh tissue from her messenger bag. The hard floor was killing Sam's knees, so she plopped down on the floor next to Joan and waited for her to compose herself. A hearty blow and a few sniffles later, Joan seemed ready to try again.

"He was there for me. Tony. I think he came back looking for me."

"Why would he be looking for you?"

"Oh lord! It's... I'm so ashamed." Joan sounded like she was about to wail again.

As sympathetic as Sam was to Joan's plight, she didn't think she could keep going through this. "Why do you think he was there for you? Did you know him?" Sam's voice was soothing.

Joan nodded.

"Did you meet him before the party?"

Joan silently bobbed her head.

"When did you meet him?"

"I met him several months ago. On one of those dating apps." Joan covered her face with her hands.

"That's a perfectly normal way to meet people. It's nothing to be ashamed of," Sam reassured her.

"But then he showed up at the party with a fiancée."

A sudden realization came to Sam. "Joan, you didn't..." Sam let the question drop away.

"No! I swear, Sam. He was already dead when I found them."

Sam sighed in relief. "I'm sorry. Please, continue."

Joan looked away, then down at her lap, where she was wringing her hands. "Our third date was a weekend in Laguna Beach. I knew it was too fast, but I told myself I needed to be more adventurous, so I agreed. The weather was perfect. We spent the day walking to different art galleries and shopping in little boutiques. A wine tasting in Laguna Canyon and dinner on a rooftop. We had such a wonderful time. The next morning, we had brunch at Las Brisas."

"Sounds amazing," Sam said.

"It was," Joan said wistfully, then her tone quickly changed. "At least, I thought it was. Later in the week, we went to dinner, and he asked to borrow ten thousand dollars—"

"Ten thousand dollars?" Sam slapped her hand over her own mouth.

"For the business, because his money was tied up overseas. I told him I didn't have that kind of money to lend. He said he understood, and I thought that was the end of it."

"I'm guessing it wasn't."

"No." The word exited Joan's mouth as a slow exhale. "Just before dessert, he was looking at his phone. He said he was looking at our photos from the weekend. I asked if I could see." Joan closed her eyes and shuddered.

Sam put one hand over Joan's. "It's okay."

Taking in a breath, Joan looked past Sam as if she were watching the memory on the wall. "He passed the phone across the table. His smile. I'll never forget it. Before I could even see what the picture was, he said, 'They say a picture's worth a thousand words. I think this picture's worth ten thousand *dollars*.'"

***

Sam was glad she'd been able to persuade Joan to come stay with her at Aunt Lily's. She'd been in such a state that Sam didn't want to leave her alone. She put Joan in the guest room and loaned her one of Aunt Lily's night gowns. Sam brought in a steaming cup of chamomile and lavender tea and set it on the nightstand. "This should do the trick."

Joan sat upright in the bed, pulling the covers over her legs and patting them down. "Do you think the detective will be mad?"

"I think he'll be glad you came forward sooner rather than later."

Swallowing her sip of tea, Joan set the cup into the saucer, now resting on her lap. "I guess we'll find out tomorrow."

"I'll let you get some sleep. Everything will be okay. You'll see."

"I can't thank you enough for your kindness, Sam. You're so like Aunt Lily, and your mother would be so proud."

The reference to her mother startled Sam, and it took a moment for her to recover. She smiled her thanks and bid Joan goodnight. It was rare when someone outside the family remembered her mother. Jennifer Gordon had died when Sam was seven years old. Sam knew she was kind, smart, funny, and beautiful, not just because those were the memories she had of her, but because her mother had left her a series of videos and letters that she would watch and read throughout her childhood. Her mom had marked them by grade, age, or milestone, and Aunt Lily or Uncle Bill would give them to her at the appropriate time. Aunt Lily gave her the video about changes her body was going through, while Uncle Bill gave her the video about dating. She had never been shy about asking questions. Poor Aunt Lily and Uncle Bill. Sam chortled at the memory.

Chapter Ten

S am decided to get an early jump on the day. She swung the door to Café Nate open vigorously, allowing the bells to jangle loudly.

"Hold your horses!" Q shouted from the back. Her expression when she came out was priceless.

"Good morning, Sunshine!" Sam flashed a Cheshire cat-sized grin.

Q looked at her watch and back up at Sam. "Girl, it's not even dawn yet. Normally, the only people I see at this hour are delivery drivers."

"Detective Finn is coming over this morning—"

"Oh really?" Q stretched out each word with a sing song tone.

"Stop. He's coming over to talk with Joan. After that, I was thinking I might check in on Abigail or Leticia."

"First, why does Detective Finn need to speak to Joan? I thought she already gave her statement. And second, bad idea."

"It's not a bad idea. It's a perfectly legitimate gesture, and I thought I would bring some fresh baked goodies from the best baker I know." Sam's cheesy grin and large twinkling eyes were doing their best to win over Q.

"I'm the only baker you know."

"That's not actually true anymore. I met bakers and cooks all over Europe."

"That may be, but none of them are going to participate in your shenanigans, are they?"

Sam jumped up and down, clapping her hands.

"Not before you tell me what's going on with Joan," Q said.

"That's going to require a caramel latte," Sam said as she walked toward the back.

Thirty minutes later, Q was helping Sam load not one but two baskets of baked goods, a cup caddy with four more caramel lattes and a little bag with a special treat just for her.

"You really are the best," Sam said, closing the trunk.

"Good luck today. You're going to need it."

***

Joan paced in the kitchen as Sam plated some of the pastries she'd picked up from Café Nate. She jumped at the sound of the doorbell.

"Deep breaths." Sam patted Joan's arm as she left the kitchen to answer the front door.

"Good morning, Detective, Officer Decker. Thank you so much for coming." Sam opened the door wide to let Detective Finn and Officer Decker inside. She led them to the living room where Joan had already laid out the pastries on the coffee table, along with napkins and plates.

"You're going to spoil us, ma'am," Officer Decker said as he and the detective seated themselves.

"This is most appreciated," the detective agreed.

"I've got caramel lattes, or I can make regular coffee."

"Black coffee is fine for me," the detective said.

"Okay. Umm, make yourselves comfortable, and I'll be back in a few minutes." Sam disappeared into the kitchen.

A moment later, Officer Decker appeared. "I thought I'd see if you needed any help with the coffee." He did a quick look back at the detective and Joan in the living room. "I also thought it might be less intimidating for Miss Harris if there weren't two of us in there."

"I'm sure you're right. Poor thing's been nervous all morning." Sam poured a quarter cup of Kona blend coffee beans into the grinder. "My coffee won't be anything fancy like yours." She poured the boiling water into the French press and over the now ground coffee. She rested the lid and walked over to the kitchen doorway, leaning against the wall.

Sam felt like a voyeur as she observed Joan talking to Detective Finn. She turned to Officer Decker, leaning on the other side of the doorway beside her. "Are you sure you don't want to hear what she is saying?"

"It's fine. I'll listen to Detective Finn's recording and read his notes." He looked at his watch. "Coffee's probably ready."

Sam bolted into action, gently pressing the plunger down, placing the French press on a tray that already had four mugs and a caddy with sugar, honey and a Stevia-monk fruit blend. "Would you mind? I'll grab some cream." She handed the tray to Officer Decker and sent him to the living room while she grabbed a carton of half & half and some almond milk and rushed to follow him.

"Sorry for the interruption." Sam placed a tray of steaming mugs on the coffee table.

"How did you come up with the money?" the detective asked, pouring several spoonsful of sugar into his coffee.

"I sold my car." Joan added almond milk and honey. "I just paid it off last year," she added, more to herself, as she stirred her coffee.

"Did anyone question why you sold it?" the detective asked.

"Not really. I told folks who asked, like Aunt Lily, that I was trying to lessen my environmental footprint. They thought it was great, like I was doing something noble." Joan sounded so dejected.

Sam seated herself next to Joan on the sofa, giving her arm a supportive pat.

"And did you pay him?" the detective asked. Joan nodded. "Ms. Harris, you'll need to verbally answer," he advised.

"Sorry. Yes, I paid him," Joan said.

Sam watched as Detective Finn lowered his head the tiniest bit to meet Joan's eyes. His voice was soft when he spoke. "Ms. Harris, I know how hard this is. These questions, and even I, sound cold and unfeeling. I want to make sure we get as much information as we can. He can't hurt you anymore, and we need to catch who committed this awful crime and make sure they don't do it again. If you need to take a break, just let me know."

Joan's mouth gave a slight upturn. "I understand. Thank you. I'm okay to continue."

The detective sat back and in his official voice continued with the next question.

"Where and when did the payoff take place?" he asked.

"It was about three weeks ago. Wire transfer. I can get you the exact time from my bank when I'm done here," Joan said.

Sam noticed Detective Finn perked up bit. "You have his banking information?"

Joan started to nod, then corrected herself. "Yes."

The detective scribbled a few words, then cocked his head slightly as he looked up and asked, "And was that the end of it?"

"I thought so. He said he deleted the photos from his phone after he got the money transfer." Joan closed her eyes and shook her head. "I don't know why I believed him."

The detective nodded in understanding, then continued to question.

"What happened?"

"I got a text from him a little over a week ago, asking for more money," Joan said.

"Do you still have the text?" the detective asked.

Joan shook her head. "I deleted it. I told him I didn't have any more money and reminded him that he deleted the photo. He replied back, saying *Technology has come so far that it does things for us automatically, like backing up photos into the cloud.* I could've killed him!" Joan's regret over her words registered immediately. "Oh dear! That was a poor choice of words. I didn't. I swear I didn't."

Sam put her arm around Joan. "Don't worry. No one here thinks you did it. Isn't that right?" Sam raised her brows pointedly in the detective's direction.

Detective Finn looked only at Joan. "Please, continue."

"I told him that we had to meet in person this time and that he had to delete the photo from the cloud and prove to me it wasn't still on his phone before I gave him the money," Joan said.

"Is that why he came back to the studio after the party?" the detective asked.

"No. I think he was coming back for more money. We had met a few days before the party. At Café Nate."

"You brought that much cash to the café?" the detective asked, surprised.

"Oh, no. I brought my laptop," Joan said, and upon seeing the detective nod, she continued. "I watched him delete the photo from the cloud, and he showed me it wasn't on his phone either, so I transferred the money to his account."

"The same amount?" the detective asked.

"Well, that's what I let him believe. Of course, when he got the transfer confirmation, it was for two thousand dollars, not ten," Joan said.

"That must've made him angry."

"He was furious at first. I told him that's all I had. I don't know why he thought I had all kinds of money. I work at an art and craft studio, for goodness sakes," Joan said.

"Did he accept that?" the detective asked.

"He seemed to, until he was leaving. Then he said he'd get the money one way or another. And he walked out." Joan's chest expanded as she took a deep inhale. "When he showed up at the party, I was terrified at first, but then he was with that other woman, and they were engaged. I thought maybe that's how he was getting his money. From this other woman." Joan cast her eyes down. "I was relieved it wasn't me anymore." She covered her face with her hands. She said with a muffled voice, "I'm so ashamed."

Sam's heart broke for Joan.

"I completely understand. I think that was probably a natural reaction." The detective was understanding, but Sam thought he was a little fidgety. Joan's head was hung so low, she didn't notice.

Sam watched Detective Finn and Officer Decker exchange looks. Officer Decker set his empty coffee mug down on the tray. Detective Finn closed his notepad and stood. *What's happening? Why do they both look so serious?* Sam jumped up, startling Joan, who looked at everyone standing, so she stood too. "So...that's some good information. Right?" Sam blurted out.

The detective was reserved. "Time will tell." He turned to Joan. "Ms. Harris, I'm sure we'll be able to verify everything you've told us." He stepped toward the door where the officer was already waiting. The two men exited onto the porch, and the detective turned. "Ms. Harris, I want to thank you for coming forward with this information voluntarily."

Sam smiled and saw that Joan was too.

"As a person of interest—"

"Person of interest?" Sam cut him off and within seconds, stood within a foot of Detective Finn. "You can't be serious!"

The detective stepped back. "I wouldn't be doing my job if I didn't issue the warning."

Sam stepped forward, closing the gap. "What warning? You just called her a *person of interest* and now there's a warning?"

"It's standard procedure, Miss G–" Officer Decker stopped when Detective Finn held his hand up.

The detective stepped forward this time, leaving no gap as Sam held her ground. He looked at Joan when he spoke, but did not budge his position. His words were slow and deliberate, but not unkind. "As a person of interest, I'd advise you to stay in town or within a commutable distance and for your own safety, I would additionally advise that you stay with a friend or have someone stay with you."

"She'll stay with us." Sam spoke quickly before Joan could protest, still looking at the detective squarely. Sam was determined not to be the first one to move, and then she could hear Aunt Lily's voice in her head, something about a tree bending or breaking. Sam heaved a heavy sigh through her nostrils and turned on her heel, leaving the detective where he stood. Joan followed her inside.

Once the door was closed behind them, Joan quietly said to Sam, "I can stay at my own place."

"Please, stay here. As much as I hate to admit it"—Sam gritted her teeth—"Detective Finn is right. I think it will be safer for you."

"You and the detective are well matched."

"What? No, we aren't!" Sam's pitch was surprisingly high. She quickly cleared her throat, "I barely know him and what I've seen so far—"

"I meant you both stand your ground," Joan said.

"Oh. Right," Sam said, feeling a bit awkward.

Chapter Eleven

S am waited in the lobby of Data Technology Systems with one of the beautifully packaged baskets of assorted cookies, pastries, and fresh muffins, trying not to dwell on earlier. She was about to offer one to the receptionist when she heard her name called in surprise.

"Sam! What are you doing here?" It was Leticia at the top of the stairs with her guest, Detective Jack Finn.

Sam's stomach dropped.

"Miss Gordon." The detective's flat tone as he descended the stairs ramrod straight made Sam nervous. His focus did not leave her.

"Detective. How nice to see you again." Sam hoped the nervous falsetto in her voice wouldn't be detected.

Detective Finn smirked as he reached the bottom and walked within feet of her.

"Is it?" He looked at the basket of baked goods, then up at Leticia.

"Thank you for seeing me this morning, Miss Pedroza." Looking back at Sam, he said, "Miss Gordon, twice in one day and the day is still young."

He turned and walked out. Sam exhaled, unaware that she'd been holding her breath. She looked at the receptionist, who made a *yikes* expression.

"Come on up, Sam," Leticia beckoned.

Sam quickly took a muffin and set it on the desk for the receptionist, who quietly thanked her as Sam hurried up the stairs. Leticia's office was light and roomy with the back wall all windows.

"Cute shoes. Tory Burch?" Sam noticed the distinctive designer's logo on the black leather ballet flat known as the Minnie.

Leticia moved behind her desk and motioned for Sam to take a seat in one of the chairs. "Sam, let me just say how sorry I am for causing such a scene at your coming home party."

"No apology necessary. Truly. I wanted to see how you were doing after everything else." Sam set the gift basket on the desk.

"That's sweet of you. Thank you, but it's... well, I don't think it's sunk in yet, to be honest. I mean, I couldn't believe it when I saw him with that other woman through the window. I just—"

"I can't imagine what that must've felt like. How long had you been dating?"

Leticia shook her head. "Long enough for me to be suckered in like some fool. What a cliché!"

"Leticia, don't be so hard on yourself. You're neither of those things. We've all dated a few lemons."

"I prefer my lemons in a martini." Leticia reached for a lemon Danish. Dipping her finger into the creamy cheese filling, she popped into her mouth for a quick taste. "Or a Danish."

"I just wanted to make sure you were okay. I imagine you had to blow some steam off after you left the party." Sam didn't think it was too obvious a question.

"You're not kidding! I think I kicked a few light posts on the way to my car."

"He's definitely not worth ruining your designer shoes over."

"Got that right," Leticia said.

Sam noticed Leticia had a tattoo on the inside of her forearm. It didn't remotely resemble Tony's, but she could use it as a conversation starter.

"I noticed Tony had a tattoo as well." Sam pointed to Leticia's arm. "Were they matching?"

Leticia didn't even glance down as she harrumphed, "Not even. Tony's was some military unit thing." She pinched a piece of Danish and popped it in her mouth. "I'm gonna have to hit the sandbag if I keep eating this."

"You box?"

"Mmm, boxing, kickboxing, a little krav maga." Leticia swallowed, licking her fingers.

"I've done a little kickboxing and it kicked my butt. Is that where you met him?" Sam continued the chit chat.

"Who, Tony? No, he was an independent contractor for us for a few months. We were up against a tight deadline, so we hired him and two others to get it pushed through. He was good. At least he didn't lie about that."

"So ..." Sam didn't know how to phrase her question.

"No, to answer the question I see on your face, we didn't start dating until after he left. We ran into each other at a fundraiser at the Bowers Museum."

Sam could see she was far away in her memory. "Sounds like you had a lot in common."

Leticia came back to the moment, her tone a little sharper. "Anything we had in common is gone now, along with the truth, lies and secrets."

"Secrets?" Sam repeated in the lightest way possible so as not to appear prying.

"Everyone has secrets, Sam." Leticia stood, walked around her desk, putting her hand out in a clear gesture for Sam to leave. "I appreciate you checking up on me, and again, I am sorry about the other night, but I've got to get back to work." Leticia seemed so unfazed by the death of her boyfriend.

Sam jumped up. "Of course. I'm glad you're okay, and I'm sorry too. About Tony."

"Thanks. I guess on the bright side, *he* didn't break up with me."

Sam didn't know how to respond to that other than to nod and smile as Leticia hustled her through the door.

Chapter Twelve

"Are you headed to the hospital?" Q's voice boomed through the car speakers.

"Not exactly." Sam quickly adjusted the volume.

"What exactly does 'not exactly' mean?" Q persisted.

"I thought I'd make good use of my time and take the other Café Nate box of goodies over to Ms. Reed."

Q sighed heavily.

"What? I'm just going to check in and see how she's doing. Like I did with Leticia," Sam said.

"And what if Detective Finn is there?"

"What are the odds? Besides, I'm already here. We'll talk later." Sam hung up before Q could object further.

Sam adjusted her visitor badge as she walked into the high school quad. It felt so small as she made her way to Ms. Reed's classroom, hoping it was in the same spot that it had been when she was a student. The lunch bell rang, and she felt like a salmon swimming upstream against a current of students making their way from the classrooms and over to the cafeteria.

Sam knocked on the frame of the open door.

"Yes?" Ms. Reed asked without looking up.

"Some things never change." Sam observed Ms. Reed making copious notes on a student's paper.

Abigail Reed's head popped up. "Sam! What a pleasant surprise. What are you doing here? How is your aunt?"

"She's doing well. In fact, she'll be coming home today." Sam set the basket of goodies on the desk and turned like she was taking a panoramic picture. The inspirational quotes that rimmed the top of the walls were mostly the same, although Sam spotted some new ones from Barack Obama and Brené Brown. The desks were arranged in U formation, just the way she remembered. Sam had loved Ms. Reed's English Lit class. It felt like yesterday and a lifetime ago.

"That must've been terrifying for her. Someone breaking in like that." Ms. Reed tapped the stack of papers on her desk to align the edges.

"Yes, well, she's still a little fuzzy on the details. How are you, though?"

"I'm fine now, but if I hadn't left town, I think I'd still be a mess. Oh, and please accept my apologies for that horrible display at the party."

"No apology necessary. Especially after everything else," Sam said.

"Yes, Tony and I clearly need to have the where-do-we-go-from-here discussion," Ms. Reed said.

"The...what?" Sam scrunched her brows, no longer sure they were talking about the same thing.

"There's no cell service at the retreat. I wasn't in the mood to argue with him while I drove back last night. The police were trying to reach me as well. I guess they're taking statements from the guests at the party."

Oh-my-gawd, she doesn't know! Sam's stomach churned and her mind raced, trying to think what she should say.

Ms. Reed checked her watch. "Actually, I'm expecting a detective any time now. I've got to meet him in the teacher's lounge." She opened the bottom desk drawer and grabbed her purse.

Sam's heart rate jumped. She did not want the detective to see her.

"Are you okay?" Ms. Reed came around her desk and held Sam's arm for support. "You look pale."

"Me? I'm fine. I should let you go——" Sam's phone dinged, indicating a text message. She glanced at the phone screen. Relief washed over her when she read the text.

"I've got to go. Aunt Lily's leaving the hospital." Sam wobbled, getting tangled in her own two feet as she tried to rush off.

"Are you sure you're okay?"

"Oh, yeah. I just——haven't eaten yet," Sam lied, eager to leave.

"Take a muffin." Ms. Reed grabbed a muffin from the basket and put it solidly in Sam's hand. "Give Lily my best."

"I will. Thank you!" Sam rushed out, careful to leave in the opposite direction of the teacher's lounge.

Chapter Thirteen

Sam pulled into Aunt Lily's driveway alongside Uncle Bill's truck just as he got out. "Perfect timing!" he said through her open passenger window.

Sam rushed to get out of her car. "If you only knew." Uncle Bill rounded to the other side of the truck where Aunt Lily waited, seat back, fully reclined. "I'll need your help after you open the front doors. Not sure I thought this through."

"Be right back." She opened the double doors and hurried back to see Uncle Bill trying to hold the wheelchair in place with his foot while he tried to slide Aunt Lily out with his arms.

"Wait! Let me hold the chair." Sam gripped the back of the chair and braced herself behind it. A few minutes and careful maneuvering, and Aunt Lily was out of the truck and into the chair.

"You got it?" Uncle Bill asked.

"No problemo." Sam turned the chair too soon. *Donk!* "Oh-my-gawd! Aunt Lily, are you okay?"

"Feeling fine, porcupine!" Aunt Lily said.

"It didn't hurt just now, when your cast hit the side of the door?" Sam asked.

"Really? Didn't feel a thing, sweetheart. Don't you worry about me."

Sam cocked a brow and sported a grin. "Those are some good pain meds they gave you." She rolled the wheelchair back to clear the truck door and spied the steps. "I think I'll let you take it from here." She stepped aside and let Uncle Bill take the wheelchair.

"Yeehaw!" Aunt Lily squealed.

As soon as Uncle Bill entered the house, he spun Aunt Lily around while doing a pop-a-wheelie.

Sam shook her head and grinned. "What am I going to do with you two?"

He stopped. "Think I'll stop before I get too dizzy."

"Killjoy," Aunt Lily teased.

"We need to get you settled in before the drowsy part of the side effects kicks in," he said to Aunt Lily. "Maybe get her some supplies to keep by her bed," he said to Sam.

"On it." Sam marched into the kitchen and started opening and closing cupboard, pantry and refrigerator doors. A short time later, she rolled a three-tier craft cart into Aunt Lily's room. On top was a pitcher of ice water, a tall glass of iced tea with a bendy straw, an assortment of trail mix, cookies, savory crackers. "I didn't know what you'd be in the mood for."

"Water is fine," Aunt Lily said, her energy level noticeably lower.

Sam poured the glass of water, transferring the bendy straw into it before handing it to Aunt Lily. "I've asked Joan to stay with us for a few days. I hope that's okay."

"She's a dear. Do you remember where the clean sheets are?" Her words sounded far away, and her eyelids blinked slowly. Her hand rested on top of Sam's, cool and soft like suede.

"I do." Sam kissed Aunt Lily's forehead, then tucked her arm inside the covers. She and Uncle Bill quietly left the room.

"You didn't tell her Joan was a murder suspect," Uncle Bill said as they walked down the hall.

"She doesn't have all her memory back yet and doesn't even realize there's been a murder. It can wait." Sam found herself squeezed into a side hug.

"I'm proud of you, kid." Uncle Bill kissed the top of her head and released her.

Sam laughed. "You're so random." She plopped onto the sofa. "I'm not sure how proud you'll be when I tell you where I've just been."

Uncle Bill sat in the chair next to the sofa. His face was expressionless as he waited for her to continue.

Sam spoke at a fast clip and finished with, "I thought I might actually throw up when Ms. Reed said they needed to have the where-do-we-go-from-here talk. That's when I got your text."

"You weren't kidding when you said perfect timing earlier." He gazed at her steadily. "So, you just wanted to check on her. See how she was doing?"

Sam held his gaze. "Mmm-hmm."

"You weren't ... snooping?"

"I mean... I can't help it if people tell me things."

Uncle Bill let out an exasperated sigh. "Because you're asking."

"Not always." Sam's impish grin spread across her face.

He leaned forward, then back again, and taking in a long breath, he stood up. "This is my fault."

"What?" This was not the reaction Sam expected.

Uncle Bill was up and pacing the length of the sofa. "I told you too many stories. Dashiell Hammett, Conan Doyle, Agatha Christie––"

"Jane Austen, Judy Blume... Heyerdahl!" Sam countered, having guessed where he was going with this. "This isn't about the books I read or the stories you told me. Or the survival tactics you taught me. Okay, maybe a little. But it's mostly about answers. And finding someone other than Joan for the police to focus on."

"Key word, police. You did the right thing with Joan. She came to you, and together you called the police. But this morning's antics border on interference--and it could be dangerous. Promise me you won't do that again."

Sam stood and gave him a tight hug, and when she pulled back, she smiled. "I promise." She scurried to the front door and hollered back, "I'll try!" She glimpsed his shaking head through a reflection in the entry mirror as she dashed out.

Chapter Fourteen

In her favorite booth at the back of Café Nate, Sam chewed on a yellow #2 pencil. She removed it from her mouth and studied it. "They need to make a bacon flavored version of you."

"Why didn't you tell me you were here?" Q held a pitcher of ice water in one hand and a plated tuna salad croissant sandwich in the other.

"I didn't want to bother you, and I really needed an escape and a place to work."

"Escape?"

"And work," Sam emphasized.

"Hold on." Q delivered the plate, refilled glasses of water and slid into the booth opposite Sam. "So, you needed an escape. Continue."

Sam regaled her with the details of her visit with Ms. Reed and conversation with Uncle Bill. "And I don't need a lecture from you too. Besides, I'm here to work." She drew out the last word.

"And what, pray tell, are you working on?"

"Take a look." Sam pushed the photos across the table.

"Oh, wow. Where did you get these?"

"Junk drawer. I found it when I was looking for one of those cheese slicer spatulas."

Q erupted in laughter. "A what?"

"The thingy that looks like a snub-nose spatula, but it's got that slit across it that cuts cheese."

Q laughed harder and tried not to snort. Sam couldn't suppress her giggle and joined in.

"I know... who cut the cheese?"

After they caught their breath, Q asked, "No seriously, why were you looking for a cheese slicer?"

"I was putting snacks together for Aunt Lily and had a flash of making a charcuterie board, but that idea was forgotten when I saw these old pictures." Sam placed another picture on the table.

"That's us!" Q said, tapping a photo of two young girls dressed in dancing girl costumes in the midst of a high kick.

"Yep. We were can-can girls for the International Talent Show." Sam fiddled with the picture. "I don't think I could do a high kick into a split anymore."

"You and me both." Q pulled the other photo towards her. "Who are they?"

"It's my dad and one of his teams."

Q studied the photo of three men and one woman, all dressed in khaki t-shirts with their left sleeves rolled above their biceps in flex poses. "This one's your dad." She pointed to the tallest man in the photo, tan and fit. "He's handsome. Do you know these other people?"

"Flip it over."

Q read out loud. "The Elementals." She chuckled. "Of course, they have cool nicknames. Hellfire, Zephyr, Me and Hydron. August '96." She handed it back to Sam and raised her brows, waiting for an answer.

Sam placed her fingertip on Hellfire's name, then held the photo side up, her finger tapping next to the man on the end. "Who does that look like to you?"

Q leaned in and squinted as if that would help her recognize him. She shook her head.

"It's him. Tony, the dead guy in the studio."

Q grabbed the photo from Sam, pulled it close to her face, then flipped it over to see the name and back around to view the photo again. "I mean, I guess it could be him. I only glimpsed him at the party."

"No, it is. Look, they must've just got the tattoos." Sam grabbed her phone, opened the camera and zoomed in, using it like a magnifying glass. "See?" The enlarged image of the tattoos was brightly colored with red raised areas around the tattoo.

"And since the guy in the studio had one, it's got to be him." Sam poked the picture for emphasis.

Q reached across, resting her hand on Sam's arm. "Hon, I know you are always eager to find stuff out about your dad, but maybe you're trying to put a square peg in a round hole. Why couldn't it be that guy? Or from an entirely different team?"

Sam bit the bottom corner of her lip. "I'm not. Look." She pointed at the other man. "Not to sound indelicate, but this guy looks white even in the desert and has platinum blonde hair."

"Sam."

"I know. I know you're looking out for me, but there's just got to be a connection." Sam's shoulders dropped. *I know there is.*

"You know I got your back." Then with a quick change of tone, she said, "And I also have a fresh, out-of-the-oven gingerbread loaf. Would you like a slice topped with my new cinnamon cream cheese frosting?"

"Uh, yes, please! And kudos on changing the subject," Sam said.

"I know, right!"

When Q sauntered through the swinging double doors into the kitchen, Sam was left with her thoughts. She was aware she tended to latch on to stories and information regarding her dad. It was a way for her to continue learning about him. There was plenty to learn. He'd had an adventurous life. Looking at the picture of the tanned, fit, dirty foursome posing in front of a camouflage net, Sam wondered what the story was behind it.

"Miss Gordon."

Sam's head snapped up. "Detective Finn! Um, what are you doing here?"

His gaze moved from her face to the photo, and she turned it over only to realize the names were exposed. She flopped her forearm on top of it then casually folded the other arm over the first and leaned forward, trying not to look guilty.

"Why did you say you were here?" Sam asked.

"I didn't say, but I'm picking up an order to go."

"Oh. Food's great here. Of course, I'm probably biased."

Detective Finn looked at her blankly.

"Q's my best friend as well as the owner. She is an excellent cook and baker. You should have one of her Danishes, and her croissants are the best, or, well, anything really. It works out well for me since I don't really cook. I mean, I can cook; it's just--"

OMG! Stop talking.

A smile broke across the detective's face. "I completely understand."

Q appeared with a thick slice of gingerbread, topped with the promised cinnamon cream cheese frosting, garnished with a curl of candied ginger, and several Red Hots candies decorated the plate.

"Q, have you met Detective Finn?"

"Pleasure to meet you, Detective. Can I get you a slice?" Q offered as she set the plate down in front of Sam.

"It looks tempting. Maybe next time. Miss Gordon was just telling me you two are friends," Detective Finn said.

"Since junior high." Q leaned over and squeezed Sam's shoulder.

"Sisters-from-another-mister." Sam smiled awkwardly.

"Are you joining Sam?" Q asked.

"Oh, no!" Sam and the detective both responded. Sam more emphatically.

"I'm just here for a pick-up––an order––to pick up an order," Detective Finn said.

"I'll go check on that for you." Q disappeared, leaving an awkward silence between Sam and the detective.

"I won't keep you. I just wanted to say hello," Detective Finn said.

"Thanks." *Thanks? Say something normal.* "Enjoy your food," Sam said with a weird half wave. He nodded and walked to the register where his order was now waiting.

Sam pretended to read a free real estate magazine. Head tilted down, she watched him through her lashes as he paid and left. He was so formal she couldn't get a read on him. She had wanted to ask if they'd found other motives for Tony's murder, but she'd become so flustered trying to hide the photo that it slipped her mind.

"You aren't fooling anyone."

Sam's heart jumped. "Girl, you are like a ninja. I need to put a bell on you," she said to Q, who slid into the other side of the booth.

"What did he say?"

"He just came over to say hello," Sam said.

"So, nothing about the case?" Q asked.

"Nope."

"And you had nothing you wanted to say to him?" Q looked directly at the photo.

Sam raised her brows, eyes searching the ceiling, and pursed her lips. "No." She put a forkful of the gingerbread loaf into her mouth and said between chews, "This is to die for."

Chapter Fifteen

S am shuffled into the living room and collapsed into a chair, letting her bag drop to the floor next to the chair. She was wiped out, and it was only 3PM. She took a deep breath and looked down at her pendant, the design matching the tattoos. Sam rubbed it between her thumb and forefinger like it was a worry stone or rosary and exhaled slowly.

At the sound of voices coming from Aunt Lily's room, Sam hoisted herself out of the chair, curious who was there.

"Look at you, out of bed!" Sam exclaimed as she gingerly hugged Aunt Lily's neck and kissed the top of her head. Her aunt sat in her wheelchair, one leg straight out because of an above-the-knee cast and the other foot, formerly on the mend, recast in hard plaster.

Joan sat on the edge of the bed, and Uncle Bill stood in the open space on the other side. Sam surveyed the room for a place to sit.

"We seem to lack adequate seating in here. Why don't we move this party to the living room?" Sam asked.

"I couldn't figure out how to get the chair down the steps without tipping her over, so I wheeled her back in here," Joan said.

Sam looked quizzically at Uncle Bill.

"I just got here before you did." He turned to Joan and Aunt Lily. "You should've said something. I can show you how to get down the steps."

Sam and Joan followed as Uncle Bill pushed Aunt Lily down the hall. Rather than try to roll the chair forward over the steps, he turned and slowly eased the chair backward down the steps, setting her gently onto the living room floor.

"I guess we better get a ramp so you can go up and down on your own," he said, locking the wheels in place.

"Joan just told me about Tony and the blackmail. I can't believe they would ever think she could be a suspect." Lily reached out and squeezed Joan's hand.

"I can't thank you all enough for your support. And I really appreciate you letting me stay here," Joan said.

"We will not give *the man* any reason to doubt your innocence," Aunt Lily said, shaking a solidarity fist in the air.

Sam chuckled. She didn't know if this was Aunt Lily's latent hippie coming out or the effect of the medication.

"It'll be good for both of you," Uncle Bill said.

"Yes! It will be wonderful to have your company," Aunt Lily said.

"What am I? Chopped liver?" Sam teased.

"You know I love your company, dear, but you're going to be awfully busy coordinating the Art and Craft Affaire with me out of commission," Aunt Lily said.

Sam had forgotten all about the event, the main reason she had come home. After winning the coveted local business sponsorship for the spring event, Aunt Lily had missed the curb as she carried a stack of boxes and broke her ankle. By the time Sam came home, her foot was in a soft-cast boot, and Sam would help in the studio so Aunt Lily could finalize the event.

"Holy cow!" Sam said. "With everything going on, it completely slipped my mind. You can just tell me what to do and where to go. Isn't that what you were going to do, anyway?" Sam asked, not entirely joking. She caught Uncle Bill sniggering.

Aunt Lily chuckled. "I'm not sure I should make calls and finalize details while I'm on pain medication, and it's only two weeks away."

Sam nodded like a bobblehead doll. "You're absolutely right. No worries, Aunt Lily. I got this."

"I have a binder with all the information you'll need." Aunt Lily pointed to the coffee table. "It'll be the next best thing to having me there."

Sam reached for the purple paisley binder on the bottom shelf of the coffee table and tried to pull it out, grasping the edge of the cover, but it barely budged. She gripped it with both hands to lift it off the shelf. It dropped with a thud onto the top of the coffee table, causing a little candy dish to rattle.

"That's heavier than my kettlebell!" Sam said.

"Nonsense. It'll fit perfectly in your bag." Aunt Lily waved her hand in the air as if to flick away the doubt.

"Only if I take everything else out," Sam mumbled to herself. She flipped the binder open. The first page was a checklist, and the next entry was Carpenter's Hardware. *Perfect. I can kill three birds with one visit.*

"I guess I better get a wiggle on." She looked at the blank faces staring back at her. "British term for moving. I better get moving." She made a big show of hoisting the binder up and cramming it into her bag, although the cramming part was not exaggerated. She swung the bag's strap over her head and across her body. "I'm off to see a man about some wood."

Chapter Sixteen

S am wandered around the lumber section of Carpenter's Hardware store. She loved the smell of sawdust. It reminded her of her dad's workshop in the garage when he used the table saw or a hand saw for his various projects.

"Can I help you find something?" The tall fresh-faced girl wore a purple vest and matching utility apron and a name badge that read, *I'm handy helper Chloe.*

"Hi, Chloe. I want to make a ramp so my aunt can move around the house while she's in a wheelchair." Sam looked around. "I was thinking of using a block of wood, cut diagonally?"

"I see. To make two triangles. Umm... If you follow me..." Chloe walked down an aisle, and Sam followed.

"Over here we have big wood cubes that might work." Chloe rounded the end of the aisle.

"I think these are too large." Sam patted the giant wood block. "I need something with a lower profile. The rise is seven inches per step and there are two steps," Sam said, looking around to see what else might work.

"Let me call one of our expert journeymen over." Chloe pulled a walkie talkie from her purple apron pocket and called for help on aisle eleven.

"Since your aunt is in a wheelchair, you'll want someone with more knowledge and experience in actual building," Chloe said.

"Thank you. You must know your stuff if you're already at Handy Helper status at your age."

"It's my family's store, so I guess I've been training for a long time." She beamed.

"Which of the eleven Carpenters do you belong to?"

Chloe laughed. "Number three son."

"He was quite a few years ahead of me. You know, I think I may have babysat you!"

Chloe blushed. "I'm afraid I don't remember."

"I wouldn't expect you to. You were all of three years old," Sam said.

"You called for an expert?"

Sam spun around when she heard the familiar Southern drawl. "Officer Decker! What are you doing here?" She took in Officer Decker's purple vest and matching apron.

"You can call me Riley, ma'am. I work here once or twice a week after my shift ends." He leaned in and added, "The employee discounts are great for someone who bought a fixer upper."

"Then you're just the person I should talk to, but please call me Sam." She thanked Chloe, who smiled and disappeared down a different aisle.

"What can I help you with, ma'am––I mean, Sam?"

Sam explained what she needed to Riley. He thought for a minute, pulled a pen and notepad from a pocket in his apron and made some scribbles before showing it to Sam.

"We could make something like this, and maybe put a grip on the sides to carry it from one spot to another."

He had drawn what looked like an upside-down set of steps.

"That's perfect. And you can make it here?" Sam asked.

"Well, no. I can cut all the pieces for you, but you would actually put it together with a hammer and nails, and maybe a smidge of putty."

It had been a while since Sam built anything. She loved projects like this, but—

Riley interrupted her thoughts. "I can come over, if you like, and make it for you."

"I'm sure I could cobble something together, but it would be nice to have someone who knew what they were doing so that it won't collapse while my aunt is trying to use it." Sam caught herself mid-ramble. "That would be great."

"Not at all, ma'am––I mean, Sam. Let's get those pieces cut for you."

No sooner had Riley walked away than Eddie Carpenter, Jr., also known as Junior, rounded the corner with arms open wide.

"Sam Gordon!" He gave her a quick hug. "Chloe said you were here because you needed a ramp for Aunt Lily."

"Junior, just the man I want to see!" Sam struggled to get the hefty binder out of her messenger bag. She finally yanked it free, only to drop it on Junior's foot. It landed with a smack on his steel-toed shoes. Sam yelped.

Junior's eyes widened. "I'd recognize that binder anywhere. Aunt Lily's got you taking over the fair."

"Yes, and I've got to get up to speed fast." Sam flipped the binder open. "I saw a tab with... here you are." She flipped to the tab marked *Carpenters* and held out the binder for Junior to review. "What's the status of these builds?" She let out a small grunt under the weight of the binder.

Junior perused the list without taking the binder from Sam or noticing that her arms were shaking from the weight of it. "Everything's on track to be finished on time."

"Great!" Sam wasn't sure what made her happier—that the craft stands would be built on time or that she could pull the binder back and stop the pain. She put check marks down the list. Now for the business she had really come for.

"Junior, during the fight at the party, you mentioned something about the man that Leticia and Ms. Reed were dating."

Junior leaned in conspiratorially. "Is it true they found him dead at the studio?" Sam's lips barely parted before he spat his next words out. "That loser. Can't say I'm sorry. Both women could do better. He's a world-class con man. I said as much to Leticia the other night."

"You told her that?" Sam's eyes widened.

"I told her she should be careful. He's not what he seems to be."

"I know you mentioned he was pretty shady when he was dealing with your dad. Was there anything else?"

"Someone who tries to skirt every legal option for payment and has an excuse for everything is trying to hide something more than bad credit. I told Leticia she should do a background check, you know, just to make sure. She's worth a lot of money now. She'd be an excellent target for someone like him. I hate to say it, but there are sharks out there."

"You're right," Sam agreed, wheels turning. *Junior made a good point. What was Tony hiding? Everyone has secrets.* Leticia's words echoed in her head.

"Here you go, Sam." Riley arrived, rolling a cart filled with cut lumber and sounding proud that he remembered to call her Sam.

"Riley, please take this to Sam's car," Junior said.

"I surely will. Sam, if you give me the keys, I'll load it up for you while you finish here." Sam tossed Riley the key fob. "It's a black Elantra GT in the aisle outside the exit."

He gave her a thumb's up as he caught it and headed out.

"Thank you, Junior. You're the best." She reached up and hugged him.

"Give Aunt Lily a big squeeze from me, and you just let us know if there is anything we can do."

"I will." Sam waved as she hustled over to the cashier.

Out in the parking lot, she came upon Riley skillfully rearranging things to make all the pieces fit like a puzzle.

"I was half expecting to have some of this strapped to the roof. I can't believe you got it all in."

"We aim to please. And there was plenty of room once I folded the back seats down. Just let me know when you want me to come over, and we'll get your aunt situated." Riley dusted his hands off before closing the hatchback door.

"Riley, thank you so much." Sam ripped off a piece of paper she'd been scribbling on and handed it to him. "Here's the address. Is tomorrow too soon?" she asked.

"Sure thing. It'll have to be the morning, though. My shift at the station starts at 1:00."

"That's perfect. How about 9:30? I'll have coffee and breakfast."

"I won't say no to that. I'll see you then." Riley gave her a crooked little smile and sauntered back inside the hardware store.

Chapter Seventeen

S am rested her chin in her palm as Q set a giant bag from the café on Aunt Lily's kitchen counter.

"You need to learn how to cook." Q pulled out a full-size quiche, a container of home fried potatoes, assorted muffins, and a bowl of fresh fruit.

"It's so much better when *you* cook." Sam knew her beaming smile wouldn't work on Q, but flashed it anyway as she grabbed plates and silverware. "Besides, I know that you brought it over personally just so you could check out the officer."

"I brought it over so I could see how Aunt Lily was doing."

"Riiight." Sam rolled her eyes.

"Is that..." Q poked at the paisley binder sitting on the kitchen counter with a serving spoon as though it would burn her. "Aunt Lily's binder?"

"Yep."

"Do you know how to use it? I can't believe she turned it over to you."

Sam stopped arranging the plates and scoffed. "It's a binder. There are lists. I make check marks. What's to know?"

"She must've been on painkillers when she gave it to you."

"Yeah. So?"

"Hon, you know how Aunt Lily is sweet and understanding, good humored and wise, with just the right amount of quirk?"

"She's the best."

"Not when she's carrying *that* around." Q tilted her head towards the binder.

The doorbell rang. Sam looked at her watch. 9:30.

"To be continued," she said and left to answer the door. "Riley, perfect timing! We were just setting out the food." Sam swung the door open wide to welcome her guest.

"Good morning, ladies." Riley inhaled as he followed Sam. "Smells like my mama's kitchen."

Q stepped forward with her hand out. "Hi, I'm Q. Nice to meet you."

Riley shook her hand. "It's a pleasure, ma'am."

"Q cooked this wonderful breakfast for us. She owns Café Nate over on First Street and Grove Avenue," Sam said.

"Oh, yes, ma'am. We order from there often. Your food is delicious," Riley said.

Q smiled at the compliment. "I'm so glad you like it."

Sam set the plate of food she'd assembled next to a glass of orange juice on a tray. "I'm going to run this to Aunt Lily. You guys start eating, and I'll be right back."

When Sam reached her aunt's room, she balanced the tray on one arm, cracked opened the door and peeked in. Aunt Lily was sitting up and smoothing out her bed covers.

"Good morning. Q brought you some breakfast." Sam entered the room and set the tray on Aunt Lily's lap.

"I wondered what was going on out there. Is Bill here too?" Aunt Lily popped a grape into her mouth.

"Uncle Bill? No, why? Oh, that's Officer Decker. He's helping me assemble the ramp for you," Sam said.

"Oh?" Aunt Lily's spoken response was one word, but her tone implied, *is this a boy you're interested in?*

"No," Sam answered, mimicking her aunt's tone. "I should get back to them, though. Is there anything you need before we get started?"

"I'm fine, dear. I'll probably fall asleep after I eat all this."

Sam kissed the top of her head before she remembered the walkie talkie and handed one to her. "I found these. If you need me, just press here and talk. Like this..." The matching unit in her pocket beeped and hissed. "It'll be our version of a bell."

Aunt Lily pressed the button. A staticky "One, two, buckle my shoe" came through Sam's pocket.

"Perfect. Enjoy breakfast, and I'll check back in a bit."

"Ten-four, good buddy." Aunt Lily's voice crackled over Sam's walkie as she left the room.

Sam returned to Riley and Q talking excitedly over recipes.

Q clapped her hands. "Riley's giving me a Jambalaya recipe I'm going to try at the restaurant."

"It's my granny's recipe. Everyone back home loves it. I know she'd be happy as a clam at high tide," Riley said.

"I'll definitely be in when you make that," Sam said, grabbing a forkful of potatoes as the coffee maker finished. "Coffee, anyone?" Sam pulled the carafe out and poured the steaming brew into the waiting mugs without waiting for an answer.

The three chatted for a bit longer about good coffee and good food before Q announced she'd better get back to the café. Sam walked her to the door.

"Thanks so much for bringing this by. I'm glad you could stay for a bit."

"It's my pleasure, hon. As my angel investor, it's your place too. You're welcome to any food you want."

"No, it's your place; thanks again." They hugged.

"I like him. He's cute!" Q hollered back as she walked out the door.

"I'll let your boyfriend Greg know," Sam retorted sarcastically as she closed the door.

When she got back to the kitchen, Riley had already put the food away and dishes in the sink.

"Your momma raised you right. Thank you!" Sam said.

Riley blushed, then slapped his hands together. "Alrighty, then let's poke the pig and get this party started."

Sam gestured for Riley to follow her. "This is where we need the ramp." She pointed to the two steps leading to the sunken living room.

Riley nodded, taking in the space before him. He whipped out a tape measure and set it next to each step. "Will you hold this end?" He handed Sam the end of the tape and walked into the living room, stopping halfway in. He checked where he was in relation to the floor-to-ceiling windows. "Plenty of space." He walked back to Sam, letting the tape roll back in. "Just double checking the measurements."

"It's a good thing," Sam said and proceeded down the hall. She opened the door and pressed the button mounted just to the side on the wall. The garage door sputtered, and the motor groaned to life as it lifted the door open, flooding the garage in daylight. Cut lumber sat neatly on the garage floor, surrounded by tools. The cars were in the driveway, giving them lots of space to work.

Riley unfolded a sketch of the ramp from his pocket and scribbled some notes on it. "Ready?"

"Ready!"

Sam and Riley moved the pieces of lumber around, on top and underneath each other, hammering as they went. After some time,

Sam stood back to survey what they'd done, arching her back and wiping sweat from her forehead. "Huh. It feels like we've done so much more."

"It's taking shape. We're nearly there."

Sam could not help herself from smiling. Riley was definitely a glass half-full person. "You're absolutely right. What should I do next?"

"Lift that corner up and make sure the side of that piece is flush, and put three nails in."

Sam grabbed a hammer and some nails. "Speaking of taking shape, how's the investigation going?"

"I'd say it's coming along."

Riley's answer was appropriately noncommittal.

Sam hammered a nail in. "Have you gathered all the evidence from the studio? Just wondering if we'll be able to re-open soon." *I hope I don't sound like I'm pumping him for information.*

"I believe they collected all the fibers and shell casings." Riley grunted as he tightened the screw on the plate.

Sam hammered the second nail and didn't realize he had continued speaking until she stopped.

"... check with Detective Finn," Riley said.

"What?" she asked.

"Check with Detective Finn!" Someone said from behind them.

Sam and Riley's heads whipped around to see Detective Finn standing like a sentinel, looking down on them from the driveway.

Riley popped up and stood ramrod straight. "Sir."

"Detective Finn, what are you doing here?" Sam grunted between her words as she struggled to stand.

"At ease, Decker. You're on your own time. I'm here to see your aunt." He perused the project, spread throughout the garage.

"I ran into Officer Decker, er Riley, when I was at the hardware store, buying wood–lumber––I was buying lumber." She swept her arm out in case he hadn't noticed.

Get it together, Gordon!

Sam took a beat to compose herself. "Riley is helping me build a wheelchair ramp."

The detective nodded, and she thought the corners of his mouth turned up ever so slightly.

"Miss Gordon, I called your aunt earlier. I believe she is expecting me."

"Of course. Let me show you in. Riley, I'll be right back."

Detective Finn looked at Sam. "I hope you aren't doing your own investigating." The detective's voice filled the quiet hallway.

"Me?" Sam cleared her throat to cover her high pitch and continued in a more level tone.

"Nooo, I was just curious about how the investigation was going. Don't worry, Riley didn't say anything he shouldn't have. He was perfectly... vague."

"That's good to hear, but I wasn't talking about your question to Officer Decker; I was referring to *your* visits to Leticia Pedroza and Abigail Reed."

Sam's blood pulsed. *Holy Cow! How does he know about my visit to Abby? Say something. It was perfectly innocent. You didn't say anything. But you need to say something NOW!*

"Here's my aunt's room!" Sam announced far too cheerily. She opened the door a crack first.

"Hi, Aunt Lily. Detective Finn is here to see you."

"That's fine, dear. Show him in." Aunt Lily sat up in her bed, her long hair in a side braid, with only the top portion of her pink and lavender tie-dye kaftan showing. She looked like a nymph in spring-time.

Sam opened the door, inviting Detective Finn in. She grabbed a chair from the corner and set it beside the bed for him to sit.

"Thank you, Miss Gordon. Ms. Phillips, thank you for seeing me. May I say you look quite well."

"Thank you. I am feeling much improved. Sam, dear, will you bring us some tea and coffee?"

"Sure thing, Aunt Lily." Sam hurried out and down the hall, popping her head into the garage where Riley was hammering.

"I'm so sorry, Riley. I'll be just a few more minutes!" Sam shouted over the hammering and closed the door without waiting for a response.

Sam filled the kettle and grabbed two mugs from the cupboard along with cream and sugar, setting it on a tray.

"This water is taking forever to heat!" Sam said, exasperated. One minute had passed. As soon as there was a hint of a whistle, Sam grabbed the kettle, pouring water into the press first, then Aunt Lily's cup where she already placed the tea strainer. She tapped her foot, waiting for enough time to go by before pressing the coffee. She couldn't wait. She needed to know what Detective Finn was asking Aunt Lily, and she didn't want to keep Riley waiting any longer than necessary either. Yeah, that was the real reason. She didn't want to be impolite. She pressed the coffee as she walked down the hall.

"Cream and sugar, Detective? Oh wait, you take it black." She corrected herself upon entering.

Startled, the detective said, "Oh, uh, actually just a smidge of both please."

"A smidge?" Sam teased. Detective Finn blushed.

Sam dropped a splash of cream and half a packet of sugar, stirred and handed it to him.

"How's this?" Sam waited for the detective's reply as she dropped the rest of the sugar into her aunt's tea and handed it to her.

After a cautious sip, Detective Finn declared, "It's perfect. Thank you."

Sam stood for a moment, waiting for them to continue their conversation. They both took another sip of their drinks and smiled at her.

"Okay then. I'll be in the garage if anyone needs me." Sam shuffled out of the room and down the hall. When she opened the door to the garage, she announced, "I'm back! Did you miss me?"

Riley looked like a shiny new penny when he answered. "I surely did. I forged ahead, though, and now we just need to sand the edges."

"Riley, it looks great! Let me grab some sandpaper, and I can at least help you finish this up."

"You did plenty, Sam. You hammered in nails like a pro. You'll be having my job at Carpenter's Hardware if I don't watch out."

"I imagine working there is a nice change from police work."

Riley was sanding one of the corners when he stopped to think about his answer.

"They actually have a lot in common. I get to help people in both. I guess that's what I like about them."

"Really? What about people like Tony?

"By finding his killer, we help you, your aunt, and if Mr. Reyes has relatives or friends, we can at least give them answers."

"Answers give closure," Sam said more to herself, but it was loud enough for Riley to hear.

"Yes, they surely do."

Sam finished sanding her side and looked up to see that Riley was finished and dusting off his jeans. She stood up and did the same thing.

"This is perfect, Riley. Thank you so much. Next time you have an afternoon off, lunch is on me."

"That's not necessary—"

"A lady offers you lunch, it's not polite to decline, Officer Decker."

Sam's head snapped around. How was this man always behind her? She was going to get whiplash.

Poor Riley was standing nearly at attention again. "No, sir. I merely meant that it wasn't necessary for her to buy me lunch, sir."

"Relax, Officer. I was teasing."

"You can see where he'd have trouble knowing that," Sam said, half defending Riley, half chastising the detective.

Detective Finn looked at Sam like he wanted to say something to her and then changed his mind. Instead, he walked past her and Riley then turned around to face them.

"Nice job on the ramp. I think your aunt is anxious to be more mobile."

"Thank you, sir," Riley said, his posture much more relaxed.

Sam felt bad, like she was one of the mean girls at school who had just shooed away someone who just wanted to be part of the group.

"You're welcome to join us." She practically shouted at him, trying to get the words out.

"That's ... thank you, Miss Gordon. Officer, I'll see you back at the station." The detective turned and walked to his car.

Sam turned to face Riley. She made the wide eyes, raised brow, with a slight grimace to ask, "Do you think I hurt his feelings?"

Riley understood because he answered. "He's okay. Honest. I know he's a little more formal than most folks, but he's good people and an excellent detective."

Chapter Eighteen

S am pulled up into Uncle Bill's driveway just as he closed his garage door.

"Hey, kiddo! Did I forget you were coming over?"

"No... Maybe I should say yes and see what you do," Sam teased.

"Hey, that's no way to treat your elders."

Sam shot him a lopsided smirk punctuated with a single eyebrow raise.

"I talked to Lily. She said you and a police officer built a wheelchair ramp," he said as they walked to the front door.

"Yes, but Riley was off duty."

"Riley?" Uncle Bill's tone was lilting. Sam punched him in the arm with one hand and closed the door behind her with the other.

"Stop it. It's not like that. He works at Carpenter's Hardware and saw me when I was buying the lumber," Sam explained.

"Hmm," was all Uncle Bill said.

"Uncle Bill! Honestly, you're starting to sound like Aunt Lily and her matchmaking set. I expect better from you."

"I'm beginning to see the wisdom of pairing," he said, plopping down a Snapple in front of her that he had pulled from the refrigerator.

"Does that mean you're interested in *pairing* with someone?"

POP! Sam opened the Snapple bottle.

He took a sip of his drink and looked at her squarely.

"To what do I owe the pleasure of your company? Although you know you never need a reason to come over."

"I know. I wanted to run something by you and didn't want to do it over the phone."

His nod was exaggerated. She wasn't sure if he was taking her seriously or being condescending. She ignored it and continued.

"Riley, Officer Decker mentioned recovering fibers and shells from the studio. I'm sure they got all the shells, but do you suppose we could find some of the same things they did?"

"And do what with them? You don't have access to a lab, and even if you did, you wouldn't know if anything you found was relevant and you've nothing to compare it to."

He continued, cutting her off as she was about to object to his objections.

"Honey, I know how much you want answers. You need to be patient. Let the police do their work." He was using his fatherly tone.

"But, Uncle Bill—"

"Sam, it's one thing to ask questions under the guise of a condolence visit, but it's a whole other thing to think you can launch your own investigation, especially when you're not sure what you are investigating."

"I want to find out what he was doing there and who killed him," Sam protested.

"No. You want to know what his connection is with your dad."

They just looked at each other in silence. Sam bit her lower lip. She didn't know if she wanted to cry or yell.

"I'm not saying we can't look into it, but let's let this investigation play out and who knows, there may be information we can use, but I don't want you to do anything that will steer the police's investigation off course or put you in harm's way."

"I'm not going to do anything dangerous."

"I know you don't intend on doing anything dangerous, but the fact of the matter is, your dad was special ops when he served and then did a lot of contract work all over the world after he and Henry started the business. So, while you think you're not doing anything dangerous, just asking the wrong person a question might be the most dangerous thing you do."

He had never said anything like that to her before about her dad. She was torn between wanting to ask more questions or hide under a blanket. She settled somewhere in the middle.

"Okay." Her answer was subdued.

"Promise?" He held out his pinky.

"Promise." She curled her pinky around his, and they shook.

Chapter Nineteen

I t was Sam's third time driving around the Plaza roundabout in Orange Grove's old town district. She was literally going in circles. She scolded herself. "Get it together, Gordon!"

She didn't know why she hadn't thought of going to see Henry sooner. She'd inherited her dad's half of the company, but she'd been so young that Henry was her proxy. She hated the idea of being looked upon as the *poor little rich girl* and distanced herself from the business even as she got older. Henry and her dad had started the security business when they were both discharged from the military.

It had been many years since Sam had been to the company her dad and Henry built. Sam's breath caught when she turned into the parking lot and saw the building. There wasn't anything particularly unusual about it. A three-story building with tinted glass window sides and a large sign along the top that said *Gordon-Hill Security*. The last time Sam visited the company, it was a listing on a directory inside the lobby. Now they had the whole building.

Sam approached a gentleman dressed in all black, wearing a headset, seated on a stool behind something that was high, like a podium but not as big as a desk, in some sort of brushed silver metal. Probably great for hiding fingerprints, but not exactly welcoming.

"Good afternoon, ma'am."

"Hi, I'm here to see Henry Hill." He began swiping on a tablet, and she quickly added, "I don't have an appointment." He looked at her like she was speaking a foreign language. "I got into town a few days ago and wanted to stop by…" She trailed off at his expressionless face.

"I'm sorry, ma'am. If you don't have an appointment, I can't send you up." His response wasn't rude, just matter of fact.

"I completely understand. Would it be possible for you to call him or his assistant to see if he has some availability?"

He hesitated for a moment, then dialed on his tablet. "Hello, sir. There's a woman in the lobby who would like to see Mr. Hill … No … Yes." He covered the mic with his hand and asked who she was.

"Sam, Samantha Gordon."

"Miss Gordon! Why didn't you say so at the beginning?" Before Sam could answer, he quickly uncovered his mic and announced to the other person, "I'm sending Samantha Gordon up to see Mr. Hill. Yes." He tapped his tablet, disconnecting the call. Hopping off the stool and from behind the podium desk, he gestured to the elevator hall behind him.

"Miss Gordon, if you'll follow me." He led the way to the elevators.

Sam glanced at his name tag. "Garvey, could we take the stairs?" She stopped following him. "It's just that I've had zero exercise since I've been back, and you know what they say, it's all the little things."

He looked confused for a brief moment, but then seemed to welcome the idea. She didn't say that she wanted to walk past the photos of her dad that hung on the walls along the stairwell. At least, she hoped they were still there.

Garvey, the security guard, and Sam walked up the steps. One side had plaques, awards, and framed certificates while the other side had pictures, including portraits of each founder. Maxwell Gordon, Lieutenant Colonel-Retired, entrepreneur, husband, father, friend.

Further on, there were lots of company photos, group pictures of departments or deployments of security detail. Sam stopped.

It was a company picnic. Sam was seven years old, sitting on her dad's shoulders, her mom standing next to him. They were laughing as they faced Henry Hill, his daughter Brittany and his wife, whose name escaped her, on either side of him.

"Are you okay, Miss Gordon?"

Sam took a deep breath. "Yes, it's just been a very long time since I've seen these pictures." She turned and started up the final few stairs with Garvey.

At the top of the stairs was a set of double doors that opened into an office. A distinguished man with silvery salt and pepper hair, dressed in a navy suit who reminded Sam of Cary Grant, stood waiting for her.

"Miss Gordon, it's a pleasure to meet you. I'm Henry's Executive Assistant, Mr. Duncan. He is going to be so thrilled to see you."

"It's been a while. I hope I'm not interrupting anything important." Sam's insides felt like jelly.

"Follow me." He tapped on the door before opening just wide enough to frame himself. "Henry, you have a guest."

"Is that so?" Henry had a wonderful baritone voice, low and soothing to the ear.

Mr. Duncan opened the door wide, stepping to the side so Sam could make an entrance, then left discreetly.

Sam stepped forward and could see that Henry was already standing with a huge smile on his face. Her apprehension melted away, and she rushed to give him a hug. He had gotten a little soft over the years, but his arms were still strong as they wrapped around her. After a moment, he stepped back, taking a good look at her.

"You look wonderful, Samantha."

"Please call me Sam. I only hear Samantha when I'm in trouble."

"Maybe that's why I forget to call you Sam," he teased.

She laughed. "I guess I did get into my share of trouble when I was younger."

"Mischief. You were never a troublemaker."

Sam looked around his office. It hadn't changed much since the last time she was there as a child with her dad.

"We came up the stairs and I saw the photo of all of us at the company picnic."

"That's one of my favorites. I have a copy of it here." He reached to the corner of his desk and flipped one of the photos around to show her. She took it from him and studied it.

"You can have it," he said.

"Oh no. That's not necessary." Sam objected, but she secretly wanted it.

"I'll have a copy made for you."

"That would be awesome, Henry. Thank you."

"I know you didn't come by just to say hi, although you are welcome to do that anytime, and you never need an appointment, nor do you need to check in with the front desk."

"You know how I feel about throwing my name around here. It would be different if I was part of the company," Sam explained.

"You are part of the company. So, tell me, partner, what's on your mind? As if I didn't know." Henry might be older, but he was sharp as a tack and kept his finger on the pulse of his community.

"You heard what happened to Aunt Lily at the studio?"

"I did." He pressed a button on his desk phone. "Eric, can you have the file brought in for Miss Gordon?"

"Yes, sir," came the reply on the other end. Henry's attention turned once again to Sam as he continued.

"Your aunt was stubborn about having cameras inside the studio, but she did agree to let us put one on the outside of the front and back doors. But we also have cameras at the place across the street and down the street at May Flowers, so I had Eric, our tech guru, compile a video to see the comings and goings of people from the party."

"That's fantastic, Henry! Thank you so much. That's more than I was expecting. Umm, I do have another question."

"Anything."

Sam took hold of her necklace, pulling it forward slightly. "Do you know the story of this?"

Henry looked at her, then her necklace, cocking his head sideways just a bit before answering. "I believe your dad had it custom made for your tenth birthday."

"Yes, but I mean the story of the symbols. I know they are elements, but what's the why?"

"The why?" Henry repeated the question.

"Yeah, why these symbols or why these elements? Why did he get these tattooed on himself and then later make a necklace for me with the same elements?"

Henry leaned back in his chair. His expression changed. She could tell he knew something.

Just then the door flew open, startling them.

"Samantha!" It was Brittany Hill, Henry's daughter and Sam's sometimes playmate when they were kids. Brittany reminded Sam of a ballerina. Lithe and graceful.

"Oh-My-Gawd, Brittany!" Sam jumped up from her chair, and they embraced like long lost friends.

"Wow, if I felt awkward next to you when we were kids, I feel like a schlump now. You look ready to take over the world." Sam gushed at her old friend, dressed in wide leg, pinstriped suit pants with a billowy white blouse tucked into the high double buttoned waist.

"Stop it. You were and still are the coolest chick in the room." Brittany motioned for Sam to sit back down. "I didn't mean to interrupt. I ran into Eric, and when I heard who was here, I told him I would bring the file."

"I'm so glad you did. It's great to see you. Aunt Lily told me you are working here." Sam turned to Henry. "You must be one proud papa."

"I am indeed. She's the hardest worker in the room."

"Daddy exaggerates, but I've made it a point to learn the basics of as many positions or departments as I can. I don't want people to think … you know."

"I totally know." Sam looked at Henry. "It's why I didn't originally give my name at the front desk."

"See, Daddy. Women are doing twice as much and tiptoeing around men's egos just to get the same respect as a man."

Henry sighed and nodded his head. "We can't fix all the world's problems in one visit. But we can help with yours." Henry's tone lightened a bit. Brittany took the hint and handed the file to Sam.

Sam opened the file and a flash drive slid out. She caught it before it hit the floor.

"There is video footage on the drive, and the documents are just the text of what you'll see on the video," Brittany advised.

Sam perused the page on top. It listed location, time of day, name, or unknown person. "Wow, you're able to identify some of these people?" Sam was astonished.

"We started using facial recognition before phones did," Henry said.

"Is it legal for me to have this?" Sam wondered if this was breaking any privacy laws.

"We wouldn't be giving it to you if it wasn't." Brittany was confident.

"We aren't breaking any laws because you are a partner, so the information is still within the company," Henry added.

"And technically, anyone using facial rec on their phones or who has even posted pictures with their names tagged has made their facial identity a matter of public record," Brittany further qualified.

"Holy cow, I never thought of that. I may have to re-think social media."

Brittany and Henry bobbed their heads in agreement at Sam's revelation. Sam stood, shoving the flash drive in her pocket, and tucking the file under her arm.

"It was so great to see you both. I can't thank you enough for this. When Aunt Lily is a little more mobile, we'll get you out to the house for dinner, or maybe Uncle Bill will BBQ."

Henry came around his desk to hug her goodbye. "That sounds wonderful. You just let us know."

Sam gave them each a quick hug and waved to Mr. Duncan as she walked out of the office.

She galloped down the stairs, stopping just before the bottom to look at the portraits one more time. *Handsome devils.* She knew Aunt Lily had these pictures in a photo album somewhere.

She reached the bottom, and Garvey wished her good afternoon as she left the building.

Sam pulled the flash drive from her pocket. "Now we'll get some answers." As she started the car to leave, another car pulled into the parking lot and parked in the guest parking close to the building. Sam had parked farther back so she could get more steps in. She would have just continued except she recognized the car and the person getting out: Detective Jack Finn. She quickly scrunched down in her seat.

After what seemed a lifetime, but was really less than two minutes according to the clock, she craned her head up to see the coast was clear. There were other cars around hers, so she doubted he would have noticed the car. Her mind was reeling. She punched the call button on her steering wheel.

"Hey, do you have some time for tea and sympathy?" This was code that she and Q had come up with when they were teens and needed to figure something out by bouncing thoughts and ideas off each other. "My place in ... thirty?"

Chapter Twenty

The kettle was heating, and Sam pulled a selection of tea out from the cupboard as well as coffee and the French press. She grabbed the walkie talkie and waited for the staticky sound after she pressed the button.

"Would you like some tea?" Sam pulled cream out of the fridge.

"I would love some Earl Grey, dear."

The kettle whistled. She poured the water into the press first so it would have time to cool a few degrees. Boiling water is the proper way to make tea, but Aunt Lily always burned her tongue. She set a tray with some cookies and pretzels since that's what was readily available, then poured the water over the basket of loose-leaf tea into the cup. Gently adding the cup of tea on to the tray, she walked back to Aunt Lily's room. The door was ajar, so she pushed it open with her foot.

"Do you want it over your lap or side table?"

Aunt Lily had a few magazines spread around her bed, but she pushed them to one side, patting her lap.

"One cup of EG and assorted nibbles." Sam set down the tray. "Q is coming over, but just squawk on the box if you need anything."

"Thank you, dear. I'm sure I'll be fine. You and Q have fun. Oh, I've been meaning to ask how you're progressing with the final details for the fair." Aunt Lily blew on her tea.

"I'm putting lots of check marks on the list." Sam overshot on sounding confident and responsible and instead it came out as forced exuberance.

Her aunt's eyes twinkled, and her lips curled up. "You be sure to let me know if you have any questions, dear." She nodded, letting Sam know she could leave.

Q was pushing the French press when Sam returned to the kitchen. "I let myself in."

"I think Aunt Lily was a Godfather in another life." Sam went to a cupboard and pulled out two coffee mugs for them. "Coffee for me too, please."

"You mean Godmother?"

"I mean like the head of *la familia*. She has a way of looking at you and smiling... I feel like I can't leave until I get—the nod." Sam used finger quotes for the last two words.

Q burst out laughing.

"You can laugh, but I'm telling you, it's a thing."

"So, what's got your brain circling the drain?" Q asked as she poured coffee into each mug, just as a timer dinged.

"What's that?" Sam looked around.

"It's the microwave. Can you grab the Danish out from there?"

"Treats!" Sam exclaimed as she smelled the buttery goodness wafting out when she opened the microwave door. A plate of croissants, some fruit and cream cheese Danish, and little quiche tarts.

"I thought Aunt Lily might like some too," Q commented as Sam set the plate down.

"You know she would." Sam pulled an assortment of the goodies aside, wrapping them up for later.

As Sam fixed her coffee, she told Q about going to Gordon-Hill and getting the file.

"What did you see, or rather who, did you see?" Q asked in anticipation.

"No one. I haven't watched it yet."

"Oh, so what's going on then?"

"Detective Finn showed up."

"What? What did he say? Wait, why was he there?"

"Ding! Ding! Ding!" Sam tapped her nose with each ding and
continued on.

"What about this would lead back to Gordon-Hill, except the tattoo. Right?"

Q sipped her coffee, brows slightly furrowed, thinking. "What
about security footage?"

"That's what I started to think too, but Henry told me she refused
to have cameras inside the studio."

"Then what is the video they provided for you?" Q asked, confused.

"They cobbled together some outside surveillance from cameras
they have installed outside other client locations."

"Is that legal?"

"Yeah, it is... but you and I are going to stop tagging each other on
social media."

"What?"

"It's a whole other thing I'll tell you about later," Sam said, waving
it off with her hand.

"What do you think it is then?" Q prompted.

"I think it has to do with the tattoo, but I'm trying not to have
tunnel vision. I need your help to eliminate other possibilities."

"The two obvious suspects are Leticia and Abigail," Q mused.

"Is being two-timed a reason to kill someone?"

"Girl, it's called crime of passion. There's a whole network of shows
dedicated to these stories."

"True." The word was more of a sigh as Sam plopped her forehead onto her folded arms resting on the counter.

"What's going on here?" Uncle Bill's booming voice didn't stir Sam from her position.

"Just hanging out," Q said.

"What's going on, kiddo?" Uncle Bill rested his hand on Sam's shoulder.

She lifted her head and pursed her lips. "Nothing."

"Sam, you promised." His voice was stern.

"What? I didn't do anything. We are just having coffee and a chat," Sam said.

"What. Is. This?" Uncle Bill grabbed the flash drive and held it out in his open hand.

"It's called a flash drive; it's basically a memory stick—"

"Don't get smart with me. What's on it?" Uncle Bill demanded.

Sam decided to lose the sarcasm and just give a straight answer. "I haven't looked at it yet."

"What do you think is on it?"

"Surveillance from the night of the party!" Q blurted out.

"Q!"

"I'm sorry. You know I crack under pressure."

"Where would you get—never mind. I probably don't want to know," Uncle Bill said.

"No, it's perfectly legal. I asked." Sam perked up in defense of her innocence.

Uncle Bill shook his head. "Let's see what's on it." He tossed the drive to Sam, who flipped open her laptop and plugged in the drive.

She double clicked on the file labeled Video. Uncle Bill and Q huddled over each shoulder. The video was dark and grainy. They watched as guests at the party entered.

"I wish I had some popcorn," Q said, eyes trained on the screen. Sam and Bill looked at her. "What? Suspense always makes me hungry."

Once most of the guests had gone in, they could see the windows get covered so anyone on the street couldn't see the inside of the studio. There were only a few passersby. Then Sam watched herself park along the curb, walk up to the door, then go around.

"Can you fast forward?" Uncle Bill asked, and Sam pressed the forward key and stopped as soon as they saw Leticia Pedroza enter the screen. Sam noticed that the cover had come down on the end window, but the door was open by then to let in some fresh air. Leticia had seen Tony through the end window, did a double take and stomped into the studio. It was only a few minutes later when she came running out in the direction she had come. Tony came out within a minute, looking up and down the street, ultimately rushing off in the other direction.

Sam felt a little queasy as she pressed the fast forward again. The next time she stopped it, would they know who the killer was?

Chapter Twenty-One

Holding her breath, eyes glued to the screen as snowy images of cars and pedestrians raced by in fast forward, she pounded on the pause button the second someone came out of the studio.

"Easy, slugger," Uncle Bill said.

"I know. I got so nervous." Sam squinted at the image. "Oh, that's you, Q." Sam pressed play and let the video go on. A moment later, Sam followed, and they drove off. "And Joan will be the next one out."

"You hope."

"Uncle Bill! Joan isn't a suspect. At least, not in my mind." Sam insisted.

"There she is." Q pointed to the screen. The headlights from a vehicle parking just out of view created an eerie spotlight as she came into view.

They all took deep breaths. Sam sat straighter and moved in closer just as Bill and Q leaned in.

No one exhaled as they watched a figure cross the street toward the studio. They could only see the back of what appeared to be a man, based on size and build. A beam of light streamed onto the sidewalk when he opened the door to the studio. The man turned his head to look down the street. It was Tony.

Sam gasped as a glimpse of Aunt Lily could be seen smiling just before the door drifted closed. Her breath quickened, and she leaned against Uncle Bill for support. When she turned her attention back to the laptop, a female pedestrian walked past the studio. Just then, the lights inside went out.

"Oh my god!" Sam exclaimed.

"Deep breath, kiddo. We already know how it ends."

Sam nodded and let out a long slow exhale. "You're right. I don't know why I'm so tense." Q gripped Sam's arm as both girls gasped. A dark figure, barely discernible in the shadows with no light from the studio, disappeared inside.

Suddenly, there was a flash.

They watched intently for more than a minute, waiting for the person to come out, when another person came into frame from across the street, running into the studio.

"Two people did this?" Sam asked, thinking out loud.

"Is that Joan?" Q asked as yet another figure walked to the door, but this time they hesitated when they opened the door.

"I think so. Look." Sam stated the obvious since they were all already looking and saw one of the people from inside run out the door, shoving Joan in the process.

Sam watched as she drove up in her car after driving Q home. She had missed seeing the person by seconds. Sam stopped the video.

"I don't understand. We saw two people go in and only one came out."

"Maybe we missed it because everything is so dark. Do you want to rewind?" Q offered.

"I wonder if we can watch it in slow motion?" Sam was rewinding back a few minutes.

"Sam, you need to give this to the police. We don't have proper tools to analyze this, and I don't want you drawing any cockamamie conclusions based on shadows." Uncle Bill used his stern voice.

"Okay," Sam replied.

"Okay?" Q and Uncle Bill chimed together.

"That was way too easy." Uncle Bill squinted at her. "What are you up to?"

"Nothing. This is just too nerve wracking. I'll definitely give it to the police," Sam said as she closed the laptop.

"I know that was hard to watch. Just remember that Aunt Lily is resting easy down the hall." Uncle Bill hugged her and kissed her on her temple. "I'm off. Be good. Both of you." He pointed at each of them emphatically then headed down the hall.

"I don't believe you," Q said as soon as he was out of earshot.

"What?" Sam opened her laptop.

"I don't believe for one second you're going to give that to the police," Q expanded.

Tapping and typing on her laptop, Sam replied, "I am absolutely going to give this to the police. As soon as it finished copying to my cloud drive."

"Samantha Gordon!" Q stood like a superhero posing. Sam stifled a laugh. "You said you were going to let the police handle it."

"That's not what I said. I agreed to give the flash drive to them," Sam corrected. Q sighed and shook her head. "And that's exactly what I'll do."

Sam pulled the flash drive from the laptop, tossing it and catching it. Her phone vibrated. The screen read OGPD. Her eyes widened, and she quickly showed the screen to Q, who covered her mouth, eyes wide, pointing at Sam.

"They know! Don't answer."

"They don't know." Sam stared at the phone.

"Then why aren't you answering?"

"I ... have... company, and it would be rude."

Q rolled her eyes. Sam bit her lower lip and picked up the phone when the call disappeared. She tilted her head and shrugged at Q.

"I'll just grab the voicemail."

"Mmm."

Sam stared at the phone, waiting for the voicemail notification. As soon as it came, she tapped it open, hit the play and speaker icon.

"Hello, Miss Gordon. This is Detective Jack Finn from the Orange Grove PD. We've got a development that we'd like to discuss with you at the station. Please call—"

Sam tapped end.

"What do you think they know?" Q asked in a hushed tone, glancing toward the hallway.

"I guess I'll find out." Sam tucked the flash drive into her pocket, slung her bag across her body and grabbed the zip hoodie from the back of the stool.

"You're going now?"

"It'll drive me crazy wondering what it is, so it's better to find out now."

"I'm coming with you." Q grabbed her purse and sweater and quickly followed Sam out the door.

***

Officer Riley Decker's face lit up with a big smile when Sam walked up.

"Hi, Riley! I got a message from Detective Finn that he wanted to see me."

"Hello. ladies, always a pleasure." Riley tapped his keyboard to make a call. "Sir, Miss Gordon and her friend are here to see you. I surely will." He ended the call and came out from around the desk. "If you ladies will follow me."

"Aren't we going this way?" Sam pointed in the opposite direction.

"Detective Finn asked to speak with you alone. I thought your friend Q might be more comfortable waiting in another room, and I could make her a coffee or something."

"You are so thoughtful, Riley. Q, you're in for a treat."

After Q was settled in, Sam sauntered happily behind Officer Decker, holding a freshly made steaming hot mocha as they went through the double doors to the detective's desk.

Detective Finn stood when they approached. "Officer, we'll be in Room 3 if anyone needs me." He eyed Sam's mug.

"Would you like me to bring you a mocha, sir?" Riley offered. He seemed to hesitate.

"Get one. It's delicious," Sam encouraged.

"That'd be great, Officer. Thank you."

Sam followed Detective Finn to an office where the small plaque next to the door read, 'Interview Room 3'. They were seated across from each other, and he pulled out his recorder, then his notepad. Sam watched, curious what she was about to learn.

"I'm going to start the recording now." Sam nodded her head, and he began by stating his name, the date and time and what room they were in.

"Interviewee is Samantha Gordon. Miss Gordon, I asked you in as we've learned there may be a link between the deceased and your family."

Sam's stomach started to churn.

"We've identified the victim as Anthony Cardoza and have discovered that this is an alias. His real name is Anthony Reyes." He paused.

Her mind raced. Her brows knit and her eyes stared at him, trying to make a connection to the information he'd just given.

"Do either of those names sound familiar?"

"No." She was still shaking her head when she asked, "Did you ask my aunt? Or my Uncle Bill?"

"Not yet. I thought I would check with you first. Has your aunt or uncle, or you, for that matter, been to Spain?"

"We all have. Uncle Bill probably multiple times. I was there...about a year ago. Is that where he's from?"

"That's where his original passport is from."

"So how do you think he's connected to my family?" Sam asked, wanting to get to the meat of it. He hesitated before starting.

"I held back some pieces of information while we investigated them further. One of those is that he had a distinctive tattoo on his left bicep. The coroner saw it when his shirt was removed. It's high enough up that even though the sleeves were short, it would've been covered."

Sam was counting her breaths—in two, out two—trying to keep her face as expressionless as possible.

"Okayyyy." Sam drew out the word so he would continue.

He slid a photo from his folder in front of her. "Does this look familiar to you?"

Sam gasped, her hand slapping her décolletage, where her pendant was tucked under her shirt.

"Are you okay, Miss Gordon?" The detective sounded worried. She took a deep breath but could only manage a nod. Looking down at her hand, she slowly pulled out her pendant, opening her hand to show him.

He stood and leaned over to get a closer look. His head snapped up just inches from her face. They stared at each other, both wanting answers. Detective Finn was the first to speak.

"Where did you get this?"

"It was a gift from my dad," she said, almost in a whisper.

"Do you know where he got it? Was it Spain?"

"No. Well, actually, I don't know. He had it made."

"Do you mind if I get that photographed?"

Sam ran her finger across the surface of the pendant.

"As long as I have it back before I leave."

"Of course." He stood and opened the door. "Officer, can you bring the camera in?" He sat back down. "It won't even have to leave your sight."

Sam unhooked the necklace and held it in her hand until the officer came with the camera. Sam set the necklace on the table. The officer produced a light box and set it up. It was like a little white stage with three sides. He placed the necklace on the platform and pressed a button on the back. The whole thing lit up. It looked like the type of photo you see for jewelry ads.

The officer held the camera directly above it. *Click, click, click.* He flipped the pendant over and snapped several angles. Sam recognized a faint *whir* as the zoom. He pulled the camera aside to look at the item and moved the little gold dangle on the clasp so that it was centered and zoomed in on that as well.

"Anything else, sir?" he asked Detective Finn.

"That'll do it, Officer. Thank you." Detective Finn removed the necklace from the lit platform and handed it to Sam. The officer was packed and out of the room before Sam could put her necklace back on, her fingers trying to find the right angle to hook the clasp in.

"May I?" Detective Finn was still standing beside her. He held his hand out.

"Oh, yes, thank you." She handed him the necklace and scooped a massive amount of hair to the side as his one hand reached around her neck.

"What is the design?" His warm breath on her exposed neck gave her goosebumps.

"Hmm?" She was momentarily distracted and came back quickly. "Umm, it's the four elements. Air, earth, fire and water."

He finished and sat across from her again. "It's beautiful." He flipped pages back from his notebook.

"So, you're the Gordon in Gordon-Hill Security."

"No. I mean, yes, but not really. That was my dad."

"But you inherited your father's half of the business?"

Sam straightened her back. "I'm a silent partner."

Sam could feel her jaw tighten. Her breath quickened. She looked at the detective squarely. He was watching her. Silent. Sam needed to be careful and not let her temper get the best of her. He was doing his job. She took a slow breath to reset and unclench her jaw.

"Is there some sort of connection with Gordon-Hill?"

He continued to study her, and Sam could swear that his eyes squinted slightly.

"Didn't your father have the same tattoo?"

Sam realized she hadn't thought this through. *I can't say no, but if I say yes...Oh my god, hurry up and say something!*

"Yes." She said it slowly, and the rest seemed to spill out. "I don't know why I didn't think of that before. I barely remember seeing it. It was always covered." That was true.

"What do you remember about it? Do you know the significance of the symbols?"

"I remember liking it a lot. I think that's why he had the necklace made." She chuckled, "Maybe he thought it would prevent me from getting my own tattoo." She smiled at the memory of her dad.

"And did it? Stop you from getting a tattoo?"

"Not exactly. I did try to get a tattoo, but it turns out I'm allergic to the ink." Sam shook her head and sighed. "It was not a pretty sight."

The detective was scribbling in his notepad as she spoke. Sam bit her lip as thoughts started to swirl in her brain.

"Detective—"

"Miss Gordon, you said before you didn't know the victim."

"I didn't," Sam answered quickly, cutting him off.

"Yes, but you didn't remember the tattoo before either."

"That's not the same thing, Detective. I think I would know if I recognized someone or not," Sam sniped.

The detective sat back in his chair, taking a deep breath.

"Miss Gordon, it's not my intention to upset you. This has become a little more complicated due to the victim's background, at least what we know so far. I'm trying to learn what I can so we can find out who did this."

Sam appreciated his soothing tone but couldn't help herself.

"I'd like to point out that my aunt is the victim. He's a casualty." She regretted it as soon as the last word left her mouth. The detective's forehead crinkled.

"I apologize. I didn't mean to imply she wasn't." His tone had changed.

"I didn't mean to say it like that." Sam clumsily tried to rectify what she'd said.

"That should be all for now. Thank you for coming in." He held the door open for her. Sam grabbed her stuff, she opened her mouth then closed it, then managed a weak, "Yeah, no problem." And scurried off.

Q and Officer Riley were chatting at the reception when Sam came out.

"I didn't want the officer to get in trouble because he was being so polite, keeping me company," Q explained their location change.

"That's nice. Bye, Riley! Thank you so much for the mocha," Sam said, barely stopping. Q hurried behind her.

"That was rude. What happened? Did he get mad when you gave him the flash drive?"

"Crap!" Sam stopped so suddenly that Q bumped her.

"Sam! What's going on?"

"I forgot. Dang it!"

"So go back and give it to him."

"No. Not today." Sam walked out.

Q ran after her. "What happened in there?"

Sam kept walking to the car, unlocked it and sat in the driver's seat and waited for Q, who got in a moment later and looked at Sam, waiting for an answer.

"He asked me about the tattoo, and I got flustered."

"Flustered?"

"Maybe not flustered. Confused."

"Confused?"

"Stop it. There was just a lot swimming around in my head and ... I promise I will give him the flash drive."

"When?"

"Soon. I just need to think through some things."

"Tomorrow, Sam. No later than tomorrow. You don't want him to find out you have it before he does," Q warned. Sam nodded and started the car. It was a quiet ride back.

Chapter Twenty-Two

S am sat at the kitchen counter, swirling a pen in circles on a blank sheet of paper. Her total lack of concentration was interrupted by a squawk on the walkie-talkie.

"Sam, are you home?"

"Yes, Aunt Lily."

"Why don't you bring us some tea and cookies or if there is anything left from the café."

A few minutes later, Sam entered Aunt Lily's room with a tray of tea and cookies.

"We ate everything from Café Nate," Sam said, setting the tray next to the bed and pouring them each a cup.

"That's fine, dear. I really just wanted to visit with you."

"Ohhh, Aunt Lily. I'm sorry I've not been here for you."

"Nonsense. I'm just bored."

"What about those?" Sam pointed to a stack of puzzle books on the nightstand.

"I've done some. I'm not in the mood. I'd rather hear what you've been up to. How are the final stages of the fair coming along?"

"Good. Mostly. Trying to pin Mrs. Whipley down is like trying to catch a whirling dervish."

Aunt Lily laughed, then immediately grabbed her side. "Umph! My ribs can't take a belly laugh yet."

"Then I won't tell you what the Tadpoles Swim School wants to do."

"Why don't you tell me what else you've been up to?"

Sam stared at nothing in particular and shrugged her shoulders. "Nothing much."

She could tell Aunt Lily was watching her.

"What's going on in that noggin?"

Sam smiled and looked at Aunt Lily. "How do you always know?"

"Nothing much always means something, dear."

Sam focused on the paisley swirl pattern on the duvet.

"I was at the station. Detective Finn had more questions." Sam sounded the way a deflated balloon looks.

"That doesn't sound encouraging."

"It is. They have new information, but..." Sam was still confused about the interview. "Aunt Lily, when did Daddy get his tattoo?"

"Goodness... early to mid 90s. Why?"

"Why do you suppose he made my necklace to match it?"

Aunt Lily's eyes sparkled and the corners of her lips curled up. "Because he wanted you to know that you were the most important member of his team, dear." She patted Sam's hand and squeezed it.

Sam rubbed the pendant with her free hand.

"What's brought this on?"

"I found an old picture in one of the junk drawers." She hadn't told her aunt about the tattoo connection to Tony because she didn't want her to worry about it, and she also didn't want her to try to stop Sam from investigating.

"Dear, would you mind taking me out to the garden?"

"Sure. Do you want some help changing clothes?"

"No. My kaftan is fine for flora and fauna."

Sam did her best to ease her aunt from the bed to the wheelchair but felt a gut punch each time Aunt Lily winced. "I'm so sorry."

"No need to be sorry. It's gone in a flash as long as I breathe through it."

She rolled her aunt out to the garden and parked her in the sun.

"I bet Bill knows."

Sam was used to Aunt Lily's hard turns in conversation—it was probably where she got it from—but she hadn't followed this time. "What does Uncle Bill know?"

"The origin of the tattoo, dear. Hello, Hilda, you look positively blushing." Aunt Lily cooed at a newly bloomed cluster of antique roses.

Sam locked the wheels, kissed the top of her head and left Aunt Lily to bask in the rose garden. She called Uncle Bill after she went back into the house.

"Hey, kiddo, what's up?"

"Hi, Uncle Bill. Are you at home?"

"No, I'm dropping off my report in person. Everything okay?"

"Yeah, all good. I just wondered if you knew the origin story behind Dad's tattoo?"

"I know some of it, I think. Sorry to cut this short, Sam. I'm walking in now. I'll call you later." He hung up.

"Okay then. Later it is. Which is fine because you have stuff to do," Sam said to the empty living room. She slid the phone into her pocket, but it wouldn't go in for some reason. Reaching in with her hand, she pulled out the flash drive. "Ah, but first I need to take care of you." Shoving the drive back into her pocket, she hollered back to Aunt Lily. "Will you be okay if I go out for a bit, or should I bring you back inside?"

"I'm fine dear. I have my phone if I need anything."

Chapter Twenty-Three

S am sat in her spot in the back corner of the café, eyes trained on the entrance.

"Why here?" Q arrived with two glasses of water she set on the table.

"Home court advantage." Sam stood suddenly, nearly stepping on Q. She waved at Detective Jack Finn, who'd just entered the café. "Hoping he'll be less likely to arrest me here." Sam straightened her posture and adopted what she hoped was a professional demeanor as he approached.

"Detective Finn, thank you so much for meeting me here." Sam made a sweeping gesture like a game show hostess.

Q gave her a side glance.

Detective Finn eyeballed them. "You said you wanted to tell me something about the case."

"Yes, please have a seat." Her voice had a higher tone and slight crackle to it.

Q sighed and shook her head. "I'll bring you both some coffee."

Sam looked at Detective Finn, who was looking at her, waiting. Sam smiled.

"Have you had the coffee? It's quite good." *OMG, why do I sound like Mrs. Whipley?*

The detective's forehead wrinkled.

"You have to try the stuffed waffles. They are to die for."

"Miss Gordon, what did you want to tell me?"

"Yes, of course, Detective." The odd affected voice was still spilling out of Sam. She took a deep breath. *Shake it off, Gordon.* Exhaling slowly, her head and shoulders shimmied quickly, getting rid of the nerves and the weird formality that had overtaken her. Leaning forward, she plopped her hand down on the table. Detective Finn waited. She pushed her hand toward him and then pulled it back, revealing the flash drive.

"What's this?"

"As you know, I'm a silent partner in Gordon-Hill Security. My dad and Henry were good friends as well as business partners." She paused, deciding how to continue. "Naturally, when he heard what happened, he wanted to help any way he could."

"And how was he able to help?" His tone sounded less congenial than before.

"Nothing illegal. I promise."

"Miss Gordon, what is on this flash drive?"

"They have several clients, including Aunt Lily, who have exterior security cameras. They put together a video timeline of the comings and goings into the studio that night."

"We've already pulled traffic cam footage. We're still going through it."

"I think you'll get more from this." She patted the drive.

He leaned in. "Do you know who killed the victim?"

"Well, isn't this cozy!"

They both snapped their heads up. Sam palmed the flash drive and Detective Finn sat bolt upright.

"Mrs. Whipley! How great to see you. Are you here for dinner?" Sam was breathless as she spoke. Whiplash grinned like a cat that got the cream.

"Mr. Whipley and I are having a date night too. At home."

"We're not on a date." Detective Finn quickly replied.

"Yeah, no, umm, Detective Finn is fairly new to the area, and I offered to tell him some of the best spots in town." Sam thought that sounded plausible.

"And what better way to do that than over dinner, at your bestie's café. I see my food is ready. Ta ta!" Whiplash Whipley turned on her heels and walked away.

They both looked at each other, breathing a sigh of relief.

"Why do I feel like I just got caught with my hand in the cookie jar?" Sam asked through chuckles.

"I know, right? Sorry, I didn't mean to make it sound like it was impossible for us to be on a date. I try to keep business separate."

"Of course. I totally get it." Sam was grateful when Q showed up with a tray of two steaming cups of coffee, cream and sugar.

"I was going to bring these out sooner, but the table looked pretty crowded." Q set the coffee tray down, dispensing everything from the tray to the table.

"Perfect timing." Sam poured cream in her coffee.

"What are the dinner specials tonight?" Detective Finn asked.

Q pulled a laminated card on a stand from the counter and set it on the table in front of him.

He read the specials aloud. "Grilled chicken pesto with sautéed zucchini, meatloaf and tots, seared—"

Sam jumped in. "Get the meatloaf and tots. Unless you're vegetarian or vegan."

"Sounds good. I'll have that," he said.

"To go?" Q asked.

"Ah, no... here, if that's okay?" He looked at Sam.

Sam stammered. "Uh, sure. That'd be great. I'll have the meatloaf too, then."

"Two meatloaf and tots coming up." Q left them for another table.

"I realized I was hungry, and we can finish our conversation over dinner," the detective explained.

"Good idea." Sam chewed on her lip. "I forgot what we were talking about."

"Did you see the killer?" He reminded her in a very hushed tone.

"Right. Yes. Well, no. I mean, not exactly." Sam looked around. "Let's go to my car." She saw the expression on the detective's face. "To watch the video. I've got my laptop." She patted her messenger bag. He nodded, and just as they both started to slide out of the booth a waitress came with their food. Sam stopped. Her stomach grumbled.

"I suppose it can wait until after we eat," she suggested. He didn't hesitate to scoot back toward the middle. She giggled a little.

"I didn't have lunch today," he said, explaining himself.

"No worries. Besides, you really want to try this hot." She watched as he took his first bite. His eyes closed and he hummed "Mmmm," as he chewed.

"I told you." Sam took her own bite to share in the yumminess.

"The meat has so much flavor."

"That's because it's a blend of beef and pork," Q announced suddenly at their table. "And my secret blend of spices. I'm glad you like it."

"I will definitely be ordering this again," the detective declared.

"The special comes with a slice of pie. We have key lime, Dutch apple and pecan left."

"Pecan," they declared at the same time.

"Good choice. I'll have your waitress bring it out when you're ready."

"Can you make the pie to go?" Sam asked, indicating she was going to show him the flash drive. "We've got to go look at something."

"Absolutely." Q gave Sam a nod as she left.

They continued to eat. Sam was beginning to feel the silence was a little awkward.

"So, where were you?"

"What?" Sam was surprised by the detective's question.

"The welcome home party, at the studio. Where in the UK were you coming home from?"

"Cambridge, and Europe before that," she answered mid chew.

"The whole of Europe?"

"Sort of. I've been traveling and working in several countries for the last few years, but Cambridge specifically was the last place before coming home."

"What do you do that has you traveling all over Europe?"

"I've mostly been an English teacher, tutor, and nanny. Occasionally, I've been a wedding photographer, event planner, bartender, and dog walker."

"That's quite an impressive list of jobs. Why not do them here?"

"I want to experience other places, people and cultures outside of being a tourist."

"It's great you have the means to do that."

Sam cocked her head slightly.

"Most people don't have the money to do that," he continued. Sam's eyes narrowed. Her lips pressed into a polite smile.

"Why do you imagine I work all those jobs?"

He stammered. "For the experience of other places and people?"

"So I can afford to have those experiences." Her words were clipped. She had to get better about becoming so defensive about money. She was grateful when the waitress came with dessert in little pie-slice-shaped containers and also set down some to-go containers.

"Ms. Quinlan said you might need these too."

Detective Finn requested the bill, to which the waitress replied cheerfully, "Ms. Quinlan already took care of the bill. Enjoy the rest of your meal." She sashayed away.

They silently packed up their food. Sam led the way out of the café.

"I'm over here." She indicated where her car was parked for him to follow. She pressed the button on the car fob and unlocked it. They climbed in, Sam setting her food in the back. He put his food on the dash as Sam pulled out her laptop.

"Miss Gordon, I'm sorry. I didn't mean to imply anything derogatory. I just meant that most people get tied up with other responsibilities—" He stopped and sighed heavily. "I'm just making it worse."

Sam continued setting up silently.

"I meant, I think what you did takes courage."

She looked up. "Thank you for that. And I'm sorry. You hit a nerve, and I have something of a knee jerk reaction." Her tone softened. She put the laptop on the center dash and pushed play.

"I've already fast forwarded to just before Joan leaves for the florist." She pointed to Joan, whose face is clearly seen as she leaves and then more shadowy as she enters the not as well-lit sidewalk. "Notice the lights are on. I'm going to fast forward." She stopped and let it play on the figure that was coming up the walk, whose features were lit as he entered the studio. She pressed pause. The detective nodded, and she fast forwarded for just a moment and let it play as soon as the figure came into view. She watched the detective as he leaned closer to the screen. Only several moments after they entered the studio, the lights went out.

"That's our killer!" the detective exclaimed.

"Wait." Sam pointed to the screen, where moments later another figure entered, then one of the figures quickly ran out, bumping into Joan. Sam paused the video.

"Only one of them ever comes out."

The detective stared at the frozen screen. "Do you have footage from the back of the studio?"

"No."

"Can we get it?"

"We?"

"You know what I mean."

"Yes, I'm sure there is footage I can get. I know your team will go over the video, but can I show you something?"

"Please."

She rewound the video to the first figure entering and played it. "It's super slight, but this person is limping. You can see it better once—there. See?" The detective nodded. "This person isn't limping, and"—she fast forwarded to the person running out, letting it play—"neither is this person."

"Good eye," the detective commented.

"You become extremely aware when you work at an embassy." Sam continued to look at the screen. "I feel like this person probably isn't the killer," Sam offered.

"Because only nefarious people have limps."

"No. I—" Sam saw the detective was smiling and she stopped her defense.

"Seriously though, you have a good eye for detail. I appreciate you pointing these out. May I?" His hand was poised next to the flash drive. Sam nodded. He grabbed the drive and his food and stepped out of the car, bending back in.

"Thank you, Miss Gordon. This is most appreciated. I'll scold you later about withholding evidence and expect that won't happen again, correct?"

Sam nodded emphatically. "Promise, and I'll send whatever is available from the back of the studio, and please call me Sam."

"I look forward to it. Enjoy the rest of your evening, Miss Gordon." He smiled and closed the door.

Sam let out a heavy sigh.

Chapter
Twenty-Four

Sam sat in her car as it filled with the aroma of fried potato and warm pecan pie. She didn't know what to do with herself. She guessed she should probably go back home and keep Aunt Lily company. She had just started her car when her phone rang, and the screen showed OGPD. She tapped the accept button. "Hello?"

"Hi, Miss, I mean, Sam. It's Officer Riley Decker," came the cheerful and friendly voice.

"Hi, Riley! What's shakin'?"

"I just wanted to let you know the art studio has been cleared so you can start to clean up and re-open anytime you want now."

"That's great news, Riley! Thank you! So, I can go over now?"

"You can go over now." She could hear the smile in his voice.

"Fantastic! Thanks again, Riley!"

"You're most welcome, Miss... Sam." And with that they both ended the call.

Sam drove straight to the hardware store and picked up a box of gloves, trash bags, some wood glue, small nails, and a hammer. She knew there was likely a hammer and nails in the studio, but she didn't want to look for them.

Sam parked in the back of the studio. As she was unlocking the door, she looked up to see the camera high above the door, under the eaves. It was really two cameras, each facing at opposite side angles. She looked around at the lot behind her.

"There are only two lights back here. I'll bet the camera footage is going to be hard to see. I guess you'll find out later." The lock clicked and she entered. She walked to the front where the mail slot was, skirting around the tape that outlined not just the dead man but Aunt Lily's chalk outline too. They wanted it for proximity and comparison. Sam remembered the officer rushing to outline her aunt as best he could while the paramedics put her on a gurney. Suffice it to say the outline shape was more blobby than human. Sam sighed, looking around the whole studio.

"I wish you had more answers." She spoke to the collage hanging on the wall. Sam turned and saw the pile of mail.

"I'm going to need a bag for you." She walked to the back and returned with a canvas tote bag and began scooping a mountain of greeting cards and notes of well wishes into the bag. She spotted a utility or vendor bill here and there, but the majority were cards.

"You all are going to make Aunt Lily's day." She stood with a bulging tote and took it out to the car. She re-entered ready to get this cleaned up before Aunt Lily came back. Gloves on and holding a trash bag, Sam carefully made her way through the studio, putting everything in the bag, even though it wasn't really trash. She would separate the items that could be fixed or salvaged from items that could be put back in their display cases, such as paint tubes, brushes, and the like. There were bits of ceramic and powdered broken glass that she definitely needed to sweep up. She stopped when she saw a shoe pattern in the glass dust. It was a big shoe. Not hers, and it was off to the side, not where she had stepped to pick up the mail.

The police, she thought, but just in case, she took her phone out and swiped for camera mode, zoomed in and snapped a few shots. Looking around, she took a 4x6 picture frame and set it down lengthwise to the footprint, with the bottom lined up with the heel.

"This will give you some perspective," she said as she snapped a couple more then moved around to the other side, careful to step over what she imagined would be other footsteps if they were in line with this one. "I'm sure you're nothing, but on the off chance— -"

"Who are you talking to?"

Sam's head jerked up to see Greg standing in the entry between the back and the shop.

"Greg! What're you doing here?"

"I saw your car. Thought I'd check in and see what shenanigans you were up to."

"No shenanigans. The police have released the studio, so I thought I'd get started cleaning."

"So, you were talking to—" Greg made a big gesture of looking around.

"I found a shoe print."

"So naturally you thought you'd have a conversation with it." Greg started to walk to where she was.

"Careful where you step. Go around that way." She pointed the direction she thought was safe for him to step.

"Are these prints only you can see?" He mocked as he looked down where he stepped.

"You'll see it when you come around."

"Oh, yeah, you're right," he said when he got to the spot she had been to previously. "But it's probably just the police, don't you think?"

"You're probably right, but just in case. May I have your shoe?"

"What?"

"Your left one. Can I have it? For comparison." She gestured to the frame.

"Why not?" Greg wobbled on his right foot as he popped his left one off and handed it to her. "Size 11."

"Good to know." She put the frame back on the table and placed Greg's shoe next to the print, heels lined up and snapped. "So, this print is probably a twelve or thirteen, right?" she guessed, handing Greg his shoe back.

"Closer to a twelve, I think," he said, popping his shoe back on. "Need any help?"

"I was going to sweep, but I might wait until after I send this to the police and see what they say, but if you want to tear down that police tape in the front, that would be great."

Sam dialed the detective's number but got voice mail. She hung up without leaving a message and dialed the police station. "Hi, Riley. It's Sam. Is Detective Finn at the station?"

"Yes, ma'am, but he's interviewing someone right now. Is there anything I can help with?"

"I may have found something. Can you come to the art studio?"

***

"You were smart to call." Riley squatted next to the footprint. "I don't think this was made by any of our guys, but we'll do an elimination to make sure." His head turned and scanned the floor, "Looks like someone entered after we processed the scene. Is this the only print you found?"

Sam shuddered at the thought. "No. There's a faint one that looks the same straight back here." Sam walked a few steps to the other print.

"There's not as much powder residue back here so it's harder to see, but I took a picture of it as well. If you have the police camera, it will pick up way more detail than my phone."

"You're absolutely right. I have it in the car. Be right back." Riley's knees cracked as he rose like a giraffe from his squat position.

"Good thing you're a photographer and know things like that," Greg said.

"I don't know if I'd call myself a photographer, but it definitely helps having spent time behind a few cameras."

Officer Decker came back and took several photos of both shoe prints and anything that resembled an indentation along the same path toward the front door.

"I sure am glad you thought about our camera, Sam. Look at this detail." Riley held the camera for Sam to see.

"May I?" she asked, wanting to take the camera from him. He nodded permission, and she pressed a couple of different buttons and zoomed into the already clear image. "That's what I'm talkin' 'bout. These DSLR cameras are so good. Check it out." She turned the display screen so Greg and Riley could see the clear, hi-res detail of the shoe print.

"Good catch, Sam. Good job, both of you." Greg cheered them both on.

"Oh no, if it wasn't for Sam's keen eye, we wouldn't have got it, so thank you." Riley piled on the compliment to Sam, which made her a little uncomfortable, and she wasn't sure why.

"Nothing like a good hunch. Let's hope it pans out," Sam said, crossing her fingers.

"I'll let'cha know. Y'all enjoy the rest of your day." Riley's southern came out, which made Sam smile.

"Wow, maybe little Miss Sherlock found a clue." Greg teased as he nudged her while they watched Riley leave.

"Ooo, sounds like Shaggy is jealous." Sam nudged him back

"Why am I Shaggy?" Greg pouted.

Sam looked up at his unruly, wavy hair that flopped just above his brows and covered most of his ears, his stubbly face, the well-worn baseball t-shirt, cargo shorts and unlaced Converse, and looked him in the eye with one raised eyebrow. "Have you looked in a mirror?"

Chapter Twenty-Five

"**M**iss Gordon, I thought you were going to contact me when you found anything regarding the investigation?" Detective Finn came from the direction of the lounge, stirring what Sam guessed was a hot cup of coffee, since the detective had already denounced mochas and lattes. She would try not to hold that against him.

"Wow, were you just waiting to pounce as I walked through the door? Let me remind you, I did contact the police. Why do you think Officer Decker was able to bring you a footprint?" Sam said.

Detective Finn took a careful sip of his coffee and then sighed heavily. Sam wondered if he was enjoying his first sip or just trying to get his frustration with her under control. She got her answer.

"Why were you at the studio in the first place if not to investigate on your own?" the detective asked.

Officer Decker came up to the registration desk just as Detective Finn finished speaking. "That's my fault. Crime Scene Investigation cleared the site and I let her know. The update is on your desk. Sorry, sir. I reckon I should've contacted you as well."

Sam thought the detective might chastise Riley and was glad when he didn't. Although, she somehow still felt a little scolded.

"No problem, Officer. Miss Gordon, my apologies." The detective's tone was so neutral, Sam wasn't sure if he'd really just let it go that fast or if he was simmering underneath. She hoped it was the former.

"Apology accepted," she answered cheerfully, hoping to lift the mood. She looked at the officer, who was smiling back at her, and then the detective, who looked at her blankly. "I was just wondering if the shoe print was helpful."

"What do you imagine we could accomplish in the ten minutes Officer Decker's been back?" The detective was back to being snippy.

Officer Decker jumped in. "I dropped it off with the tech team. They'll take it from here."

Sam felt awkward. She wanted to suggest something, but worried she would further incur the detective's wrath, so she stood there. Looked at each man. One smiling, the other resembling a straight-faced emoji.

"Alrighty, then. I will leave you to it." She took a couple of steps back before turning toward the exit as the officer bid her to have a good day and the detective merely said, "Thank you."

Once outside, Sam said in a very mocking tone, "Thank you. Thank you for not getting in the way. How about, thank you for finding evidence we didn't find? Or thank you for getting additional video. How about—"

"I'm sorry."

Sam spun around, heart thumping, to see Detective Finn a few feet behind her. She gulped what felt like a tennis ball then opened her mouth to say something, anything, but the detective held his hand up. "Let me apologize. I didn't mean to sound like I was reprimanding you. And you did do exactly as I asked. I was just concerned that you were putting yourself in harm's way again."

Sam pressed her lips together and blinked in confusion. Her first instinct was to hand him a sarcastic reply, but luckily, her better angel took over. "Thank you, Detective. I appreciate your apology."

He nodded and turned to walk away. She could've been home free, but the better angel must've flown away. "It's not like I do it on purpose," she blurted. He stopped, turning to face her. "Things just come to me."

"Things? You mean cockamamie ideas?" He walked back to her. "I believe you. I believe you have so many of these *things* flying at you that it's a wonder one of them hasn't killed you yet."

"I'm not going to apologize for the fact that I have an open mind. You should try it sometime. I'm not going to limit—"

"An open—there are procedures in place for a reason. This isn't one of your cute little investigations from high school or some debutante's stolen tiara at whatever embassy. This is a murder investigation and—"

"You don't think I know that?" Sam yelled and continued as she stepped closer to the detective. "You're only investigating a murder though, aren't you? I need to know why he was there. Did he intend to do harm to my aunt? What's his tie, if any, to my dad, or to me? Who is the person threatening us, and are they working separately or were they his accomplice? Why is this"—she grabbed her necklace—"suddenly so important?" She was out of breath and could feel her eyes well up. She blinked them back, not wanting the detective to see them.

The detective stepped forward, further closing the gap. His intensity and volume matched hers. "All of that is part of our investigation. Which is exactly why I need you to steer clear." He softened suddenly. "I can't also be worried about you getting hurt or worse."

Sam chewed the inside of her lip deciding how to respond. "I understand what you're saying. Really, I do. But someone is threatening my family. Has already hurt my family. They're all I have, and as much as I'd like to put your mind at ease and say I won't get involved anymore, I also don't want to lie to you. And I don't want to keep having this same argument. I promise, anything I uncover or comes to me, I will tell you." Sam didn't realize she was gesturing with her hands and arms until her arms dropped when she finished.

The detective sucked in a breath. "Be discreet. Be careful. And don't do anything questionable alone. And I promise, we won't stop until we've found answers to all those questions."

Sam clasped his hand between hers in earnest. "Thank you." He covered her hands with his other hand and gave a quick nod. His hands were warm and reassuring. Sam thought she noticed gold flecks in his eyes, making the green more striking. It reminded her of the cat she had when she five. The cat's eyes were stunning. How had she not noticed this before? OMG! How long had she been staring into the detective's eyes? She quickly stepped back, breaking their hands apart.

"I better let you get back to work," she sputtered. "Let you catch those bad guys," she added awkwardly. She thought she caught a little smile on the detective's face before she turned to take the rest of the steps to her car. Unlocking the car, she quickly got in and made an exaggerated turn while grabbing the seatbelt to see if he was watching her. She was relieved to see he wasn't and was nearly back inside when he turned around and waved.

"Oops! Smile and wave, Gordon. Be breezy." Just as she waved, she realized he wasn't waving at her when another man in uniform walked past her car waving and saying something to Detective Finn.

"No problem. He probably didn't see you anyway. Just drive away," Sam said, coaching herself, wondering why she cared.

Chapter Twenty-Six

"Hi, Brittany, it's Sam Gordon... Good morning to you too. Hey, I was wondering if you could check any cameras in the back of the studio on the night of the uh-murder from 9:55 to 10:05? Email is perfect, and if you wouldn't mind including the detective... that'd be great." Sam was sipping her coffee when the walkie squawked.

"Good morning, Sunshine!" came her aunt's voice.

"Good morning to you too. Are you ready for some Earl Grey and scrambled tofu?"

"That would be wonderful, dear."

Sam made scrambled eggs for herself. Tofu was not something Sam could embrace, despite her aunt's efforts.

They finished eating in her aunt's room. Sam collected the dishes onto a tray.

"Do you want me to park you in the garden while I'm out?"

"I think the living room today. I want to catch up on my stories."

"Okay, be right back."

Sam set Aunt Lily up in the living room with a foot stool and an ice chest filled with drinks and snacks.

"I'm just running errands, so it won't be too long. Call me if you need anything." She kissed the top of Aunt Lily's head and headed out.

"Sam! Could you swing by the studio and pick up the mail?" Aunt Lily shouted.

"Oh! I can't believe I forgot. Hold on."

Sam showered the cards over Aunt Lily, turning the tote upside down.

"What's all this?" Aunt Lily held her arms out to catch them as most cascaded on to the floor around her.

"Your mail."

"Oh, my goodness," was all she could say as she opened one that settled in her lap.

The crayon drawing on the front looked like it was maybe a teddy bear holding balloons, or maybe they were just large colorful polka dots. "Read it out loud," Sam prompted.

"'Roses are red, violets are blue, get well soon, we miss you.' Isn't that the sweetest?" Aunt Lily looked around. "You better help me, or I'll never get through these."

Sam picked up a neatly folded piece of lavender construction paper. On the outside, in purple crayon, it was addressed to 'Miss Lily' with a picture of a butterfly made from tiny footprints. She turned it around to show Aunt Lily. Sam opened it and read.

"'Dear Miss Lily, I'm sorry you got hurt. I had to stay in the hospital for a tonsil icky and got ice cream and Jello. I hope you get ice cream and Jello too. I hope you get better soon and don't hurt anymore. Love, Jasmine.'" Sam laughed and turned the card to show the picture of an ice cream cone and what Sam could only imagine were flowers.

"That's adorable, Aunt Lily." Sam bent over and grabbed another folded sheet. It had a pencil drawing of a bunch of daisies on the front, but when she opened it, there was a skull and crossbones, also drawn in pencil, and in block letters it said, "BACK OFF OR AUNT LILY WON'T BE SO LUCKY NEXT TIME!"

"What does it say?"

Sam quickly folded it up and shoved it in her pocket. "Nothing—it's a note to myself that must've fallen in, but that reminds me that I do need to run another errand. I will leave you to revel in your cards and be back later." She stood and scooped up some cards from the floor, placing them on the coffee table in front of Aunt Lily and started to rush out.

"Bill is taking us to dinner tonight so be back and ready to go by 6:30."

Sam hollered back "Okay," as the door closed.

***

Sam's first stop was Gordon-Hill, where she dashed in, and a small, padded envelope waited for her.

"Gordon-Hill. Check. Next stop..." Q's name and face flashed on her phone. She tapped to answer. "Hey, girl, whatcha doin?"

"Just got through with the morning rush and wanted to see what happened last night."

"Nothing much. I showed him the video. Pointed out a few things and gave him the flash drive."

"And he was okay with it? It looked like things got intense for a bit at dinner."

"That. That wasn't about the drive. He said something that pushed a button. I reacted, like I always do, and he accepted my apology."

"Okay, that's good. What about the other?"

"The other? Oh, he was pretty cool about it, although there was reprimand in his tone, and I promised I wouldn't do it again. In fact, I was going to go grocery shopping but"—she eyed the envelope sitting

in the passenger seat—"maybe I better go deliver the latest information."

"Yes, do that first. I'll chat ya later."

***

Sam dialed the police station as she backed out and tried not to speed.
She cut Riley's greeting off before he got through the second word.

"Riley, is Detective Finn available yet?"

"Miss Gordon? Is—"

"I'm on my way in and I need to see him right away." Sam's voice
was raised in urgency. Officer Decker clearly picked up on it.

"I'll make sure he's aware. Sam, is there anything I can do?"

Sam felt comforted by his offer. "No, Riley. Thank you. I'll see you
soon." She knew it would only be a matter of minutes and could just
show up at the station, but she didn't want to wait.

No one was at the reception desk when Sam walked up into the
police station. She could hear muffled yelling through one of the office
doors. It became loud and clear when it opened and Officer Decker
came through, closing it quickly. He was at the desk in a few strides.

"Hi, Miss Gordon. How can I help you?"

"I thought I'd gotten you to call me Sam?"

"Miss Gordon is more appropriate at the station."

"Fair point. Lots of commotion back there."

The detective is the one interviewing someone right now."

Sam perked up. "Is it a suspect in my case? I mean my aunt's case?
Who is it?"

Officer Decker looked around. "I'm not at liberty to tell you."

"Riley, you know I'll find out anyway. I can just stay here until they leave, unless he's arrested, in which case it becomes public record."

He looked back at the doors. He looked genuinely distraught. Sam thought about letting it go when he leaned forward and whispered. "It's my boss. From the hardware store."

"Junior?" Sam exclaimed, then quickly lowered her voice. "That's ridiculous. Why would they even think...?" Sam kept shaking her head as if the answer would tumble out.

Riley continued in a whisper. "His fingerprints were found at the victim's office."

"That's—no. I'm sure that's easy to explain."

"What's easy?" Sam recognized the stern baritone, and so did Riley, who bolted upright. "Officer, will you bring the interviewee some water, please, while I see what Miss Gordon is here for?" Detective Finn stood behind Riley.

The officer couldn't escape fast enough. The detective stepped up to the reception desk. He opened his mouth to speak, but before he could, Sam slapped down the envelope in front of him.

"I brought you this. It's the footage of the back of the studio."

"Were you able to identify anyone?"

"I thought we could look at it together."

He looked back at the door. "This is likely going to take some time."

"That's fine. I can come back later, or you can call me when you're done. And I'll leave this with you." She slid the envelope towards him, eager to make sure she was holding up her end of the bargain. He took the envelope.

"I'll call you. Thank you for this." He held up the little envelope. Sam nodded as he walked back. Riley hadn't returned yet, so Sam decided she'd better get on with her day.

***

The day had consisted of countless errands and the last one was finished. Sam buckled up then reached into her pocket expecting to find her lip gloss and instead pulled out the note she'd hidden from Aunt Lily's mail. She had one more stop.

Detective Finn was waiting for her at reception when she arrived. "What's happened?" the detective's voice was concerned.

"With everything that happened here earlier, I forgot to show you this." Sam pulled out the note, handing it to him. "This was in my aunt's mail from the studio today, but it's clearly meant for me."

He read it and flipped it over to see if there was anything else. "When did it come? How did it get in with the mail?"

"There's a mail slot in the front door of the studio. There were a bunch of handmade get-well cards that came through the slot, along with the regular mail. I just picked it up for the first time since all this happened."

He finished what she was thinking. "So, it could've been left any time in the last few days."

"I'll call Gordon-Hill and see about getting footage," Sam said.

"That's a good start. Who have you been talking to?"

"No one! Just the same people you have. Probably."

He looked skeptical.

"I paid my condolences to Leticia and Abigail. Junior actually volunteered information. You aren't still holding him, are you?" He scowled so she finished. "And, of course, Q and my family."

"It may be someone who was within earshot. There were several people around when you were talking with Mr. Carpenter at the hardware store," Officer Decker chimed in as he joined them.

"True, but there wasn't anyone around when I visited Leticia or Abigail. I guess there might have been a student or two, but with all the noise, I doubt they heard anything, and even if they did, all they heard about was a fight at a party."

"There's someone we're overlooking. There's definitely two distinctive people that enter your aunt's studio." Detective Finn dropped the note into a plastic evidence bag.

"So you looked at the back footage?" Sam asked.

"Not yet. We just wrapped up with Junior and let him go." The detective made a point of punctuating the last three words.

"I knew it." Sam beamed. Officer Decker smiled, and the detective smirked.

"We can look at it now if you've got time." Detective Finn offered.

"Yeah!" Sam walked past them toward the double doors without waiting for an escort.

***

Sam and Detective Finn sat close behind his desk to view the monitors. Officer Decker brought them a couple of bottles of water.

"In case you get thirsty."

"You're so thoughtful. Thank you, Riley—I mean, Officer Decker." Sam smiled and winked. He blushed and walked away.

"I think someone has a crush on you."

"What?" Sam looked at Detective Finn queuing up the new flash drive video.

"I've never seen him so attentive to anyone before."

"Riley and I are pals," Sam said cheerily.

Detective Finn shot her a side glance. "If you say so."

"I do. Say so."

"Okay, let's see what we got."

The video played. Sam was right. The lighting wasn't very good. The exit door was in the middle of the two lights and only got crossover light spill. She hoped it was enough. They had watched a blank screen for a couple of minutes when the figure popped into view. Sam's breath caught. They both leaned forward. Detective Finn double tapped the play arrow so it played in slow motion and they could see it frame by frame. Again, they could only see the person from the back, but this time, they could tell this person was wearing a hoodie with the hood up, and once they were far enough forward, they could see the figure walked with a slight limp. Sam gasped, grabbing the detective's forearm. They looked at each other, Sam raised her hand for a high five.

"Is this weird? I feel like it's a small celebration."

He chuckled and gave her a high five. "It definitely gives us something to focus on. Are there any other cameras in the back?"

"No." Sam sighed, the victory already fading.

"I expect to have the traffic cam footage tomorrow. We may be able to cross reference with someone wearing a hoodie now." Detective Finn sounded hopeful.

"Thank you for letting me see this with you." Sam slung her bag over head.

"It's probably less dangerous that way, and you brought it to me, after all." He stood.

"It's okay. I know the way out, and you're busy." She started to walk away.

"Miss Gordon, I'd refrain from discussing anything in public areas."

She gave a nod and a smile in agreement. Deep in thought as she exited the station, her fingers moved across the pendant, feeling the texture of the design.

She would go see Henry Hill in the morning.

Chapter Twenty-Seven

"I need you to tell me everything you know about this picture." Sam reached across the desk, handing Henry the photo.

Henry studied the picture. "The Elementals. Your dad was pretty proud of this little ISO unit. He used to say that this unit could do anything."

"What's an ISO unit?"

"International Special Ops."

Sam's eyes widened. "That's the man that was killed in Aunt Lily's studio." She leaned forward, tapping Tony's image. "Was he from Spain?"

"Tony?" Henry's voice shot up in surprise.

"I wonder why they called themselves that. I thought the Elementals were bad guys. At least that is how they come off in comics. Don't you think it's odd he didn't introduce himself to me at the party?" The questions spilled out of Sam's mouth.

"Well, unless you were introduced as the daughter of Max Gordon, I don't imagine he knew." He set the photo on the desk and leaned back in his black leather chair. "You know, I have no idea where he went after he left us."

"He worked here?" Sam's tone was a mix of surprise and frustration.

Henry's calm expression only served to make Sam feel more manic. Questions that seemed impossible to answer filled her head. She heaved a weighty sigh with her plea. "Henry, I need to understand what's happening and what it all means."

He nodded. "Of course, Sam. Our resources are at your disposal." His words were reassuring. Even though she was a partner in the company, she never considered it hers.

Henry pressed a button on his phone. A male voice came over the speaker. "Good morning, Mr. Hill."

"Good morning, Eric. Could I ask you to take a break and come to my office?"

"Of course, sir. Is there anything you need me to bring?" His voice was strong over the hum and electronic chatter in the background.

"Just your presence. Thank you." And Henry hung up.

Sam felt sorry for Eric. That would be a nerve-wracking call to get first thing in the morning.

"Anything I or the company can do to help untangle this for you, we'll do."

"Thank you. The police are doing fine, it's just... well, Uncle Bill said there are two investigations, and I think he's right."

Henry gave a knowing smile just as there was a light tap on the door. "Come in."

"Good morning, Mr. Hill!" Eric's enthusiastic greeting didn't match his tentative entrance. He reminded her of a slightly older Clark Kent with a sprinkling of salt and pepper around his temples, which set off the black-rimmed glasses.

"Have a seat." Henry gestured to the chair next to Sam. "This is Samantha Gordon. The video you compiled was for her."

"Oh, nice to meet you." They shook hands, and he sat down, asking, "Was the video helpful or is there a problem with it?"

"It was very helpful, and please, call me Sam." She turned her attention to Henry, eager to discover why Eric had been called in.

"You were working here at the same time as Tony Reyes, weren't you?" Henry asked.

Sam snapped her attention to Eric.

"Tony? Yeah, I started a year or so after him. I mean, he did field work, and I did operational support, but yeah, our paths crossed a few times on the job." He paused for a minute. "Actually, I just saw him a few months ago."

"You did?" Henry and Sam chimed in simultaneously.

"Yeah, he moved to the area and is starting his own security consulting business or something like that."

"Did you talk on a regular basis? What's the name of his business? Do you know where it is?" Sam stopped when she saw Eric's wide eyes and raised brows. "I'm sorry, each new piece of information sends a series of questions exploding in my head."

"I don't think it's public knowledge yet, but"—Henry leaned forward, directing his comment to Eric— "Tony was the man found in Sam's aunt's studio."

"Understood, sir. If I may ask, how did he die?"

"He was shot." Henry sat back in his chair.

Sam bulldozed over the answer into her next question. "Did he talk about personal stuff?"

"Nah. We might have talked sports a little, but we were never close like that when he worked here. We mostly talked about equipment. He wanted to know what I recommended."

"Prior to a few months ago, how long had it been since the last time you saw him?" Sam's inquiry went on.

"Man, like"—he looked at Henry— "whenever he left here."

"I'd have to look it up for an actual date, but that would be about fifteen years," Henry said.

"What was Tony like back then?"

Eric looked up at the ceiling, then down at the floor, as if reading a giant invisible document. "He was part of a team of contractors." He glanced at Henry, who nodded for him to continue. "He followed through on instructions. Knowledgeable. Got the job done. Liked his tequila."

Sam interrupted what was sounding like qualifications for a job application, except for the part about the tequila. "When you say contractors, you mean a part of a security team you hire out?"

"That's right," Henry said.

Sam nodded her understanding and continued, "What about his temperament?"

Eric shrugged his shoulders. "He seemed pretty even keeled, although I guess there were a couple of times I saw him get in people's faces about little things. Maybe not little, but his reaction didn't match the situation."

"Can you give us an example?" Henry beat Sam to the question.

"He did it to me once. His team had just completed their assignment, and while they were in transport, the comms—that's short for communication devices—started acting up. Going in and out until they were out for about three minutes. But as I said, the mission was over, and they already had their exit information and were on their way. When the comms came back on, he was going ballistic, and the others were yelling at him to calm down."

"What was he going ballistic about?" Sam asked.

"I couldn't tell at first. Everyone just seemed to be yelling at each other, and I finally got them quieted down enough to ask what the commotion was about. Before anyone else could say anything, he started going off about the comms, but not in a normal way."

Sam cocked her head, bidding him to continue.

He scooched to the edge of his seat. "It's important to understand that when the comms went offline, there was no imminent danger, no mission instructions being given. It was just chatter, like you would have if you and some friends were in the car driving somewhere and you had someone talking on the car speaker."

"Irritating but not earth shattering," Sam said.

"Exactly! Except Tony went off at me, yelling at the top of his lungs. I get it. A minute in the middle of a mission, things could go bad, but that's why we also have local comms—so they can still communicate with each other. Like I said, the reaction didn't really match the situation."

"You've been with the company a long time then," Sam observed of Eric.

"He's one of our best," Henry bragged.

"Thank you, sir." Eric sat taller, and Sam thought he might have even blushed a little.

I have a million questions for this guy. "Eric, would you mind if I got your number and have the detective contact you?" Sam asked.

"Of course." Eric pulled a card from his pocket and handed it to Sam. His gaze lingered on her. "I had the pleasure of working with your dad. He was one of the best mentors and humans I've ever known."

The sting in her chest caught Sam off-guard. She sucked in a breath and quickly blinked back the moisture welling in her eyes. "That's so wonderful to hear. It means a lot to me. Thank you. And thank you for taking the time for all of this." Sam looked at Henry and stood. Both men followed suit.

"Thank you, Eric," Henry said, and Eric departed. Sam watched him leave as Henry appeared beside her, putting his arm around her shoulders.

"He was also the best partner and friend anyone could ever want."

Sam leaned in, letting her head flop on Henry's chest, nodding.

Chapter
Twenty-Eight

"**Y**ou better stop pushing your food around the plate, or I'm going to think you don't like your breakfast." Q leaned on the opposite side of the counter at Café Nate and watched Sam not eat her corned beef hash with a side of extra crispy bacon and an apple spice muffin.

"The food is great, Q. I'm just trying to sort everything out in my head."

Q walked to the end of the counter and reached under the shelf below the register. She came back with several kids' menus and crayons. Sam looked at the items placed in front of her.

"You know I love to color, but I don't think I'm in the mood right now."

"No, silly." Q flipped the papers over to the blank side and grabbed a crayon, holding it out to Sam. "It's so you can make your lists and charts. I didn't have any extra pens or pencils, so... here you go, and multi-colored, so, you know, make a rainbow chart of suspects."

"We did this already," Sam whined.

"Yes, but you know it makes you feel better, and there's been new information since the first time. Maybe it will jog something." Q pushed the items closer.

"You're probably right." She sighed and picked up the green crayon and drew a giant T on the page. Along the top, in block letters, she wrote *suspect* on the left and *motive* on the right.

Q looked around the nearly empty café and pulled up a stool from behind the counter as Sam changed to an orange crayon. Under *suspect* she wrote: *Leticia, Abigail, Junior*, and a big question mark.

"Who's the question mark?" Q asked.

"The runner who bumped Joan."

"You don't think it could be Junior?"

"He has an alibi, but I want to keep all the names up here for now." She finished the list with Mr. And Mrs. Carpenter. Switching to the purple crayon, she scribbled motives next to the names. *Jealousy, betrayal.* Sam tapped the crayon on the paper leaving little blue dots. "Pretty weak, isn't it?"

"I didn't want to say anything but, yeah." Q continued to study the sad little list. "What about something like protection for Junior?"

Sam nodded in agreement. "Right. Protecting his parents from any further money scams." She added to her motive list and continued writing. "And money could be the motive for the Carpenters."

"I can't even begin to imagine that. Did you add them just so you could have something to cross off the list?"

"I know they are just too sweet." Sam drew a line through their names then added a question mark. "Just in case."

Q slapped her palms onto the counter and stood. "Don't be mad, but I can see why Joan is the police's prime suspect."

Sam's shoulders slumped as she let out an audible exhale. "I know. It's not lost on me." She reluctantly wrote Joan in the suspect column.

Q stepped into the kitchen and returned a moment later. "Sorry, I've got a giant pot of stew simmering for tonight's special. Geez, that looks ominous." Her fingernail grazed the waxy words next to Joan's name.

"If you've got something more accurate than fear and desperation for motive, spill." Sam dragged her crayon through Joan's name. "Even if the police haven't crossed her off their list, I can cross her off mine."

"I don't know what Junior's alibi is, but the police seemed to have accepted it. Abigail didn't even know he was dead, so..." Q interjected before Sam could cross out the last name.

"That could've been an act. Wouldn't you pretend not to know that your two-timing, conniving fiancé had been murdered on the same night you had a huge public cat fight?"

"Good point, but she stopped at the grocery store near her house. The camera shows her entering and exiting the store during the time frame he was killed. She couldn't have made it back to the studio." Sam drew the line through Abigail's name.

"I suppose Leticia's alibi is solid as well?" Q asked.

"Yeah, one of the outside cameras shows her storming out the door and kicking the lamppost as she walked up the street. The bartender at Duke's verified she was there until closing." Sam crossed off Leticia's name.

"So, we're back where we started," Q said bleakly.

"I guess I should find out where the Carpenters were. You know, just to make sure." She scribbled a note in crayon to herself. "We've made a little progress."

"Where?"

"If all the known suspects have alibis, then there are two people who entered the studio that night, and we don't know who they are. Right?" Sam's tone was oddly cheerful.

Q looked at her friend and shook her head. "Only you would find that uplifting."

Sam drew blue crayon swirls on the paper. "It makes me happy that no one we know is a murderer... but it means we still don't know who is," Sam added somberly. "The more I find out, the more I think it has to do with Tony's past."

"What makes you say that?"

"Something they said at Gordon-Hill."

"All the more reason you should just leave it to the police."

"Yeah, yeah." Sam rolled her eyes.

The bell jingled on the café door, and the mail carrier set an unruly stack of mail on the counter and waved at Q, "Sorry it's not tied together. Just got knocked over by a guy walking and texting. Ought to be a law against that."

"No worries. Thanks, Dave!" She jumped off her stool and waved as he went on to his next delivery. She rifled through the stack as she walked back to Sam.

"Anything good?"

"Nah, just the usu--"

"That must be interesting." Sam watched her friend freeze in her tracks.

She pulled a sheet of paper and handed it to Sam. "One of those question marks knows who we are."

"What?" Confused, Sam took the unfolded paper. The outside was blank, but when she opened it, she saw the pencil drawing of skull and crossbones and read, IF YOUR LITTLE FRIEND DOESN'T STOP POKING HER NOSE WHERE IT DOESN'T BELONG, THERE MIGHT BE AN ACCIDENT AT THE CAFÉ.

"Oh my god, not you too!" Sam's head whipped around, looking everywhere in the café. "This was in the mail. Is there an envelope?"

"What do you mean, *me too*?" Q tossed her the envelope. "It's blank. What do you mean? Did someone else get a note like this?"

"Aunt Lily. Well, it was with Aunt Lily's mail when I picked it up from the studio yesterday, but the message was clearly meant for me."

"And you're just now mentioning it?" Q's pitch was high enough that the couple of patrons turned to look at the pair. In a more hushed tone, she continued, "You can't keep these a secret. I'm calling the detective."

"You're absolutely right," Sam said as she dialed her phone.

"I am?" Q's shock was genuine.

"Detective Finn, it's Sam Gordon. Yes, another note just came in the mail. At the café. We'll be here." Sam ended the call and looked at Q. "He's on his way."

Q stared blankly. "Who are you and what have you done with my friend?"

***

Sam had moved to the back booth by the time Detective Finn arrived at Café Nate, and Q had gone to her office to file away the regular mail from earlier.

"Miss Gordon."

Sam looked up from the papers she had been scribbling on and motioned for the detective to sit. She slid the papers over to the side except the note and envelope that were in a clear plastic freezer bag and slid it in front of him.

"Thank you for coming. Q and I both touched it, and, well, with food and drink around, we thought we better protect it."

"I appreciate it." He flipped it over then back again. "No drawing on the outside this time. The block print looks similar, and it has the same skull and crossbones."

Sam nodded at his observation just then Q arrived with two mugs and a glass of water on a tray.

"I didn't know what you'd be in the mood for. Coffee, tea or water. Or if you'd prefer, I could bring iced tea or lemonade."

"Water's fine, thank you."

Q set the glass of water in front of the detective and quickly placed the tray on the counter, coming back to slide in next to Sam before he could take his first sip, eager to listen.

Detective Finn took his pen and notebook out. "So, was it on top of the mail stack?" Detective Finn asked Q as Sam shook her head as she too, looked at Q, who answered.

"It was in the middle in an unmarked envelope. That's why it caught my attention."

"Was it your regular mail carrier?" he asked. Sam nodded, and Q answered.

"Yes, it was Dave. He's been delivering mail here for years."

Detective Finn scribbled in his notepad. "Did either of you see anyone approach him before he entered?"

Sam and Q both shook their heads as Q looked at her unusually silent friend. "You look like one of those bobble head dogs on a dashboard."

"I was trying to let you talk and not interrupt," Sam said in earnest.

Detective Finn cracked a little smile.

"See. Even he knows," Q said, spying the detective.

"Whatever. Oh, wait. He mentioned he was knocked over by someone texting and that's why the mail wasn't bundled. But we didn't see it." Sam redirected her attention to the detective. "Do you think you'll be able to figure anything out from this?"

"You never know. The smallest thing can break a case. That's why it's important to report ev-er-y-thing." He was very deliberate with his last word.

Sam threw up her hands as Q stifled a snicker. "You know everything I know now."

The detective looked at the papers shoved to the side of the table. "And are we teaching Mystery 101 to preschoolers?" He held up the crayon scrawled sheets of suspects and motives.

Sam snatched the papers from him, crumpling them into a ball. "It's my process."

Detective Finn sighed. "You don't need a process, because it's being handled by the police. Professionals who know what they're doing and can protect themselves."

"I'm just gonna..." Q slid out of the booth and the conversation.

"Look, I'm sorry I didn't tell you about the tattoo right away, but you know now, and I brought the first note to you immediately, didn't I? And I get it, I'm not the police, but I can't not try to find out who tried to kill my dad. I mean my aunt." She took a breath. "She's everything to me."

Detective Finn seemed to be studying her. "I understand. Really, I do. I can tell you have a curious nature. All I ask is that you keep me informed and don't act on anything."

"I promise."

He nodded, grabbing the note as he slid out of the booth. Sam slid out too.

"Burn that," he said, indicating the crumpled suspect list. "I don't want that falling into the wrong hands."

"Thank you so much for coming, Detective," Q said from the counter.

"Yes, thank you," Sam reiterated.

He nodded. "Please be on the lookout for anyone unusual and report it. Enjoy the rest of your day, ladies."

They watched him walk out, and as soon as he did, Sam pulled out her phone and tapped on it. "Hi, it's Sam again. I'm so sorry to ask for more video, but—" Sam gave a time frame before and after the postman came and asked for front and back footage of the café. "Yes, email is fine. Thank you so much, Eric."

"What do you need that for?"

"Remember, Dave said somebody bumped into him and the mail scattered."

"You promised to keep the detective in the loop from now on," Q said in an accusing tone.

"And I will. Once I know if there is anything to loop him in on," Sam said defensively.

"What am I going to do with you?"

"Pack me up some goodies to go for Aunt Lily? Pretty please and thank you."

Chapter Twenty-Nine

S am popped a piece of spearmint gum in her mouth as she made her way to Ms. Reed's classroom. Her breakfast hadn't been particularly smelly, but she didn't want to take a chance on her breath. The campus was empty except for faculty and administration. Sam loved those random days off from school. A loose locker door creaked in the breeze and some locks pinged and scraped against doors. She hadn't realized how eerie the school grounds were with no kids around. She shook off the shiver as she lightly tapped on the open door to Ms. Reed's class.

Her eyes were red and swollen, and she pasted on a smile when she turned to answer the knock. "Oh, Sam. What are you doing here?" She plucked a tissue from its box and blew hard.

Sam wanted to run and pretend she never suspected her favorite teacher of anything bad. What was she thinking? "I thought I'd see how you were doing. Someone mentioned they saw you at school."

Ms. Reed sniffled. "I couldn't stay home. His things...I thought today would be a good day to work. Keep busy... I know it doesn't look like it, but it's been helpful." She waved the used tissue, still in her hand.

"Is there anything I can do to help?"

The teacher shook her head and burst into tears. Sam rushed to her side and rubbed her back. "I'm so sorry. I shouldn't have come."

Ms. Reed's words were warbled and came between sobs. "Sometimes... I don't know... if ... I'm crying because ... I'm sad ...or because I'm mad." She raised her head and looked at Sam. "Do you have any idea how humiliated I was to find out he was dating another woman while we were engaged? And she was younger, and a former student, and it all got aired in public." She heaved a sigh so heavy she slumped onto her desk.

"I am––so––" Sam stumbled for something to say.

"I did wish for something bad to happen to him." Her eyes welled with pregnant tears ready to spill. "But I was thinking skin rash or food poisoning—coming out both ends ..." The tears flowed.

Sam leaned down and hugged her tight. There was no doubt in her mind that Ms. Reed was innocent. If the worst payback she could think of was Montezuma's revenge, she wasn't exactly a murderer in the making.

Ms. Reed's shoulders stopped shaking. She gently pulled away from Sam and straightened herself in her chair and looked at the papers on her desk. "I don't know what to do." She yanked another tissue out and dabbed her eyes.

Sam knelt and gently swiveled the chair toward her. "I know this is probably the worst timing, but I've discovered that ... Tony may also not have been the most—um—honest businessman."

"I guess I'm not surprised at this point," Ms. Reed said.

"Did he ever mention if he was having trouble with anyone? You know, in the course of getting his business off the ground?"

Ms. Reed shrugged her shoulders. "If he did, I don't recall. Oh, but we were out to dinner last week, and he had an argument with another man. I think it was the owner of the hardware store."

"Mr. Carpenter argued at your table?"

"No." She reached for a new tissue. "They were in the hall that leads to the restrooms. They got loud. The manager rushed over to see what the matter was. Tony came back to the table, and when I asked him what it was about, he said he didn't want to ruin our nice dinner and changed the subject." She sighed and looked into Sam's eyes and grasped her shoulders. "I always knew you were special." She pulled Sam into an embrace.

Sam didn't know what to say as her head pressed into Ms. Reed's midriff. She said a muffled thank you and eased out of the embrace and stood up. "I should let you get back to work."

"Thank you for letting me cry it out. I'm sure I'll be better now."

Sam stopped at the door. "Just let the tears come. If you hold them back, they just build up until the dam breaks." Sam walked to her car. She set the leather messenger bag on the passenger seat and buckled herself in. She untangled her hair and necklace from the shoulder belt and caressed the pendant as she looked at it. "This isn't about you, is it?" Heaving a sigh, she started her car. "We need to look at this with fresh eyes."

Chapter Thirty

S am yawned as she hoisted three easels from the supply area in the back of the studio onto her left shoulder, grabbed three large flip charts with her right hand and marched out to the front. It was an early start to the day. She kept the window shades down. She didn't want anyone to see her inside. As she was setting the easels up in the spacious middle, where Aunt Lily held classes and demos, she heard a bang on the back door and Q's muffled voice.

"Hellooo, I come bearing coffee and pastries."

"It's unlocked! Come on in!" Sam hollered back.

"Sorry it took longer than expected. Some guy backed out of a parking space and into the delivery van." Q hoisted a carton dispenser of coffee and boxes of pastries onto the check-out counter.

Sam stopped setting flip charts on each easel. "What? Someone tried to hit you?"

"No, no. It was an accident. The van was parked cattywampus and my driver ran in for the last box. Nothing even happened to the van." She crossed her heart for emphasis. "Oh, boy! You either have a long list of suspects or you plan on writing really big." Q set the coffee and pastries on the counter and walked over to Sam. "I hope it's the latter."

"I just want to be able to get down everything we know so far. I feel like it's all jumbled. I can't get it straight in my head. Can you grab those markers?" Sam finished, pointing to a table on the other side of Q.

Handing them to Sam, Q said, "It doesn't actually need to make sense to you. As long as it makes sense to the police."

Sam gave her the pursed lip, half-raised brow look that meant, 'Oh please!'

"What was I thinking? Look who I'm talking to," Q teased.

Sam chuckled as she walked over to the counter. "But first, coffee."

"Right behind you. The creamer is in the Thermos."

"This seems like a lot of coffee for the two of us," Sam noted as she prepared her coffee.

"Greg is joining us."

"Great! The more brains, the better."

"Glad to hear it. Is there enough coffee for me?" Uncle Bill appeared from the back.

"Uncle Bill! What are you doing here?" Sam set her coffee down and gave him a quick hug.

"I called the house to see if you wanted to grab breakfast, and Lily said you'd left for the studio already. I thought I'd better come by and supervise whatever mischief you were up to," Uncle Bill said.

"No mischief. Just hashing some stuff out," Sam said.

Uncle Bill looked at the blank flip charts and nodded. "Well, okay, then. Like you said, the more brains the better."

Twenty minutes later, after coffee and some pastry, each flip chart had names of victims, suspects, alibis, and possible motives. The top name on the center chart was Joan. Sam stood back surveying the names.

"We've got to dig deeper into these others to find who might have had an equal motive. Joan didn't do this," Sam said.

"What we need is someone with the same or better access than Joan had," Greg said.

"Right. Joan is their prime suspect not just because of her possible motive, but because of the timeline," Uncle Bill added.

Sam surveyed the flip charts. "We need more suspects. There's something we're missing." They each quietly contemplated the colorful charts.

Greg was the first to break the silence. "Do we know if he blackmailed anyone else?"

All eyes turned to Sam, whose face looked as blank as theirs until she exclaimed, "That's it! He needs to be on this board as well." She grabbed a red marker and wrote TONY in the open space below Joan's name.

"We need to know more about him." Sam scribbled what she knew. *Real last name - Reyes; from Spain; served in military - international ops unit; blackmail, two-timer, con-artist.*

"Who did he con?" Uncle Bill asked.

"Junior told me Tony was trying to get Ed Senior to front him supplies with a shady story about his funds being tied up overseas. And I think he might have because they had a heated argument at the party," Sam said.

"What about overseas?" Q asked. "Is there a way for us to find out if anything similar happened there?"

"Let me see what I can find out," Uncle Bill said.

"He didn't just start blackmailing people in the last year of his life. There's got to be a trail," Q said.

"Exactly," Sam agreed, her eyes scanning the flip charts. "I bet we can still find more victims and suspects close to home."

"You can add us to the list."

They spun around to see Mimi and Gigi standing in the doorway. Sam managed to close her gaping mouth but wasn't sure the surprise was gone from her face. "Oh, no! I'm so sorry. Was it blackmail or something else?"

The twins shuffled toward the group, and Sam rushed to meet them, hooking her arms into theirs as a way to show solidarity and compassion. They were greeted with warm pats on the back and hugs of empathy from the others in the group.

"It was blackmail." Gigi scanned the flip charts and made a guttural sound. "He did the same thing to me as he did to Joan. Risqué pictures. I mean they weren't rated X or anything like that, but he threatened to send them to my parents--"

Sam gasped.

"Right?" Gigi continued. "I would've been disowned but only after my mother survived her heart attack and my dad killed him to save my honor." She shook her and shrugged her shoulders. "I didn't have a choice but to pay him."

"But why would we add both of you to the list? Did he do the same to you too?" Sam asked Mimi.

"No. He blackmailed me over Gigi's pictures--"

"Which I didn't know about," Gigi interjected.

"Because he knew you'd protect her," Q said.

"How can someone be such a scum bucket?" Sam cupped the sides of her head and threw her arms in the air. She paced with force. "Seriously. Are people born that way or are they made?" Her eyes bored into Uncle Bill.

"Sweetheart, unfortunately it's both. Girls—I hope it's okay to call you girls since you're like daughters to me—men are... I don't know but I promise, some of us are good. Your father is a wonderful man. Greg is a wonderful man." He pounded Greg's back.

"Well, I doubt anyone is shedding any tears over this guy." Q smacked the flip chart with Tony's name on it.

"That's for sure." Sam sucked in a slow breath and chewed her lip as she looked at Mimi and Gigi. "But now you are definitely suspects. Have you told the police?"

"We wanted to tell you first," Mimi said.

"Yeah, we should have said something right away, but it took us a minute to admit it to each other, so I only just found out about Mimi this morning," Gigi said.

"We wanted to make sure you knew. And we would never do anything that would have put Aunt Lily in harm's way." Mimi's warbled voice and watery eyes gave way and Sam rushed to embrace her. Gigi joined in and then everyone else did too, forming a hug huddle. Once they peeled apart, Sam stood staring at the flip charts.

"Do you have alibis?" she asked.

"I do, but she doesn't." Gigi tilted her head toward Mimi, who raised her hand sheepishly.

"Well, out of the two of you, it's good that you have an alibi," Uncle Bill said. "Although family reputation can be a strong motive."

Sam wrote the sisters' names in the suspect column with blackmail written next to them in the motive column. "What's your alibi, Gigi?"

"After we left the party, I went to my boyfriend's. I probably didn't get home until after midnight."

Sam jotted down *boyfriend* and the time under alibi. "Mimi, what about you?"

"Gigi dropped me home, and I didn't go out after that. I watched part of a movie with my mom, but she went to bed when it was over." Her eyes traveled up searching her brain. "I think it was nine o'clock. I couldn't even tell you the name of the movie, I was so freaked out."

Sam stared at Mimi without seeing her. She brainstormed for an answer to a question she didn't know.

"Do you have a land line? Did you make any calls?" Q asked.

"We do, but I didn't use it," Mimi said.

"Oh!" Sam exclaimed and pulled her cell phone from her jeans pocket. The others waited for more. "Yes, it's not great, but it's something." She triumphantly turned the phone to show the others Mimi's social media feed, but they all stared blankly at it.

"I just see a couple of pictures from the party," Uncle Bill said.

"Look what time they were posted." Sam tapped the screen. "Nine forty-three! It must take at least fifteen minutes to get from their home to the studio, right?"

"Unless she drove like a bat out of--"

"Greg! We're trying to construct an alibi, not break it," Q said.

"It's okay. We need to cover all the angles," Sam said.

Gigi perked up. "One time we were late for dinner with my dad and his client. Mom drove like a crazy lady--"

"Oh, and she even ran a yellow light!" Mimi chimed in.

"And it still only shaved off a minute. I pointed that out since I kept telling her to slow down," Gigi finished.

Sam made a note on the chart of the social media post time and the estimated drive time. "I know it's not the strongest alibi, but it does put your arrival time outside of the window."

"But she could have made the post from anywhere," Greg said.

"I had the car though," Gigi said.

"They'll just say she used another car," Sam said.

"No, that's the only car right now. It's Daddy's car. We sold ours last year to lessen our carbon footprint and Mommy's is at the shop getting reupholstered." Mimi perked up.

"That's great!" Sam scribbled *no other cars* next to Mimi's alibi. The triumph was short-lived. The silence was only awkward for a moment. "Do you want me to go to the police with you?"

"No, we'll be okay, and now we're ready. Right?" Gigi squeezed her sister's hand. The twins hugged everyone before they left.

"Never would have seen that coming," Q said.

"Ms. Reed, Leticia, Mr. Carpenter, Joan, Mimi, Gigi... There's more out there." Sam stepped back and scanned the flip charts with names and circles and arrows in different colors. It looked like abstract art.

"I've got to run to the hardware store and pick up an order. I'll see if I can find anything else out." Uncle Bill kissed Sam's forehead and left.

"Thanks, Uncle Bill." Sam watched him leave. "You know I had a story in my head that Tony had come back to the studio because of my dad, or even me. And that he wanted to tell me something, I don't know what but something about my dad, and he was just at the wrong place at the wrong time." She stepped closer to the charts and shook her head.

"Oh hon. I'm sorry." Q sidled up to her friend and patted her back.

"No, it's fine. I mean, geez, this guy was not a good person. After seeing Ms. Reed and trying to find a ghost car, I think I know that the whole tattoo and him being in the same unit as my dad is just a coincidence and nothing to do with what happened." Sam straightened her posture and sucked in a deep breath. "We've got a murderer to find."

***

Sam found herself alone in the studio as the others had gone on their own information gathering missions while she decided to stay and check out her own ideas. She hopped off the stool. "Holy cow, here's another one." Grabbing a marker, she added another name to the growing list of victims slash suspects.

"Who are you talking to?" Q blew on her nails as she walked through the back door.

"You're back! Well, while you went for your mani-pedi, I had the brilliant idea of taking the photo that Joan sent me of Tony and uploading it to my social media to see if it automatically tagged him, and it did!"

"You posted his picture?" Q pulled a face.

"No, I didn't actually post it, but you know how it tries to identify the face when you first upload it? Each time I got a slightly different name. Then I would go to that profile page and sure enough, there he'd be with another woman. So, I'd go to her page—well, some were private, but you get where I'm going." Sam made a show of tapping the marker on the additional names.

Q stood with her arms crossed as she studied the list. "That's ... crazy. But how do you know they were all blackmailed?"

"Well, I don't know for sure, but these are the ones who had ominous postings on their pages about relationships that were dated after the lovey-dovey pictures of them together. I know it's not exactly scientific."

"Trust your gut." Greg came up alongside Q and kissed her on the cheek.

"Where did you get off to?" Q asked.

"I sometimes run into Junior at the batting cages."

"And did you?" Sam asked.

"No, but I talked to the manager, and they mentioned Junior was in last night. He bought thirty tokens and used them all."

Sam cocked a brow, and Q raised her forehead.

"That's over two hundred pitches. That's a man working out some issues," Greg said.

Sam put an asterisk next to Junior's name. "I barely made it swinging at ten pitches. That's both impressive and disturbing."

"Where did all these names come from?" Greg asked.

"More victims of Tony," Q said.

"Which means more suspects." Sam made a big star next to two of the new names. "They were both here. At least, they were probably here. Based on their posts. See?" She turned her phone so they could see a photo of two kids completely covered in sand on the beach in front of the Santa Monica pier with the caption "First time seeing and being in the ocean!" posted the day before the incident.

"That's not exactly here. Where is she from?" Q asked.

"Nebraska. Okay, how about this?" Sam tapped a couple of times and whirled the phone around. "This is next door."

Three twenty-something women wearing various princess costumes with tiaras stood in front of a round glass horse-drawn carriage. The photo was captioned "Me and my girls celebrating a quarter century like the princesses we are! Woot woot!"

"That was just two days ago, and prior to that..." She scrolled the same feed so Q and Greg could see the princesses had been nearby for over a week, posting from Laguna Beach, San Juan Capistrano, doing a great job visiting Southern California.

"So, in your scenario, a girl gets jilted, and she stalks him. When the time is right, she enlists her girlfriends to go on a trip, and between the sightseeing and amusement parks, she hunts him down and kills him?" Greg said.

"I would do that for you," Q said.

"Me too!" Sam squealed.

"You two frighten me." He backed away and waggled his finger at both of them.

"It may not be her but look at this list! And these are just the ones we know about." Sam picked up a cheese Danish, tore the corner off and popped it in her mouth. "We need to think of a way to draw them out."

"No. I think this list proves we should leave it to the police. Plus, what if that fender bender with the café delivery wasn't an accident even though it totally was? Isn't that all the more reason to give this information to the police?" Q said.

"You were in an accident?" Greg sounded alarmed.

Q shook her head. "A guy backed out of his parking space and banged into the corner of the van's bumper. It barely got a scratch. The rear bumper of his car is toast though."

Sam turned back around and scanned the charts as she tapped the capped end of the marker against her chin and muttered to herself. "I just need one good idea."

***

It had only taken the afternoon for Sam to think of a plan, and she could hardly wait to regale her best friend with it.

Q leaned across the table in the back booth at Café Nate and emphasized each word. "This is the worst idea––ever!"

"Or is it the best?" Sam's eyes twinkled.

"No. It's definitely the worst." Q fell back against the seat and crossed her arms.

Greg arrived and scooched in next to Q. "Hey, babe." He kissed her cheek. "What's the worst?"

"Nancy Drew over here has a cockamamie idea to draw the murderer out."

"You're going to set a trap?" Greg clapped his hands.

"Shhh!" Sam peered around. The café was all but empty. "It's not really a trap. I have an idea for a post on my social media that *if* the person saw it, they would show up at the studio."

"You're setting out bait," Greg said.

"For a trap." Q over-enunciated her words.

Sam rolled her eyes and sighed. "Look, it's no different than marketing."

"Excuse me?" Q asked with incredulity.

"I'm advertising a special on a product to get people into the studio. That's Marketing 101," Sam said.

"Oh my god. Remind me to never hire you to advertise the café."

"What's the bait?" Greg asked.

Sam leaned in. "Aunt Lily said Tony was extremely interested in the framed collage."

"You took those photos too." Q slid an elbow onto the table.

"Yes, but she said Tony was more interested in the frame and asking questions about it." Sam chewed the inside of her lip, Greg looked at the ceiling and Q swirled her finger on a burn mark in the Formica table.

Sam broke the moment of contemplation. "Anyway, since he kept asking about it, wanting to see it even though it wasn't for sale, I thought I would post a picture of it on the studio website as well as my social with the caption 'Taking this beauty off the wall and delivering it to its new owner.' With me standing next to it."

"That's good. Create a sense of urgency," Greg said.

"Right?" Sam said.

"No. Not right. And you, do not encourage her." Q waggled her finger at Greg, who grimaced then promptly winked at Sam. "Did you give the list of potential suspects you found on social media to the detective?" Q asked.

"I did."

"Then why not just let them handle it?"

"Have you met me?"

"I'll help and be there to back you up." Greg stared down Q's glare. "She's going to do it anyway. This way we can make sure she isn't alone and has some backup."

Q threw up her hands. "Fine."

Chapter Thirty-One

S am pushed the door open to the All Souls Art & Craft Studio with her hip. One hand gripped a baseball bat from her one sad attempt at softball with the door keys dangling from her pinky while the other hand balanced a large pink box. She leaned the bat against the wall, then set the box next to the register. "Times like these I wish I was an octopus." She wiggled her arms in the air. Her phone rang, putting an end to her little dance. "Hey, Greg. Are you on your way?"

"I thought I would pick us up some stakeout snacks."

"Great minds. I brought a pink box full of fried and filled yummy goodness."

"Yesss. Okay, I'll bring the salty treats then. You want a soda or anything?"

"Water, please."

"You got it. I'll be there soon."

Sam put her phone to silent and slid it into her pocket. She gave it a pat for security. Wandering around the studio, she looked out the window and caught a glimpse of May Flowers locking the door to her florist shop. "Hmm..." She reached up on tip toes and pulled the window shade down and proceeded to do that with all the windows and the door. "Let's give you a little jiggle. Locked." Sam squinted. "It's a little too bright in here." She moved back to the light panel and pressed the switch labeled *front*. "You need to look closed like the other shops on the street. Let's flip you and maybe you too." The switches labeled *studio* and *register* were also turned off. Only the light from the back spilled in just enough to see the pink box of donuts. "Much better. Ooh, I better grab the jelly before Greg gets here." With the tips of her fingers, she gingerly lifted a plump donut dusted with sugar and checked for the tell-tale jelly dot at the insertion point. She cupped her free hand underneath the other; her tongue licked her lips in anticipation of the sweet juicy bite that was suddenly interrupted by the sound of shattering glass.

Sam dropped the donut and crouched down behind the check-out counter. Pieces of glass tinkled against the other shards already on the floor. She couldn't tell if the thud she heard was the deadbolt being thrown or her heart pounding in her ears. *Breathe, Gordon, breathe.* Her hand grabbed the bat on instinct, clutching it close to her body, quickly using it to reach the light switch and flip off the back lights. "Oh crap." She just hoped she wasn't bringing a bat to a gun fight.

Just stay hidden and dial 9-1-1.

She glanced at the back door, dialed the police and immediately turned the volume off.

I hope the line stays open.

Orange blossom scented air rushed through as the front door creaked open and broken shards of glass clinked against each other as they were being shoved aside. Her breath quickened. She peeked around the edge of the counter. A dark, shadowy figure stepped into the studio. Her heart raced.

This is your last chance to get out.

Sam jumped up, gripping the bat and charged the shadowy figure. Using the bat as a battering ram, she slammed the intruder to the ground with a thud. "Stay where you are. I've called the police and I'm armed." She was impressed with how forceful she sounded.

"Unless that's a double-barrel shotgun you're pointing at me, I think you're the one who better stay where you are."

Sam knew the voice of the would-be burglar. "Leticia!"

Leticia groaned, holding her middle with one arm as she got to her feet while her other hand aimed a gun at Sam. It wasn't pointed at her chest or head, but Sam wasn't thrilled about the possibility of getting shot in the abdomen or thigh. She wished she had a double-barrel shotgun; not that she'd know how to use it, but it might make this a little more even.

"Leticia, I don't understand. What are you doing?"

"What I am doing is finishing the job my stupid boyfriend couldn't."

"What job?"

"I wish you could see your face. You look like one of those puppies cocking their head side to side. They look so cute, but they're just too stupid to understand what's going on around them."

Sam needed the wheels in her head to kick into high gear.

"You and Tony? You sent the notes?" Sam felt her brows knit together.

"I don't have all night. Get up the ladder, Gordon, and bring down that picture." Leticia motioned with her gun for Sam to move. They walked over to where the rolling ladder was.

Sam bumped the ladder on purpose, making it roll several feet.

"No funny business. I go to the shooting range at least twice a week." Leticia waggled the gun.

"No funny business. It's just dark." Sam walked a few steps and reached for the ladder, rolling it back.

"Here, I don't want you falling in the dark. At least not with the picture." Leticia turned her phone light on and shined it up the ladder.

Sam carefully placed her foot each step, trying to think how to stall. She'd shoved the phone in her pocket, hoping the line was still open and that a 9-1-1 operator had sent the police to do a wellness check. When she arrived at the top, she purposefully reached for an oil painting mounted next to the collage.

"How stupid do you think I am? The other one."

"What's the big deal about this picture? It's not worth anything." Sam had carefully turned to face the framed collage that contained a set of four photos she'd taken at different times in her life. "These are random pictures I took."

"You really are clueless, Gordon."

Sam struggled to lift the heavy collage off its French cleat. Her dad had created this beautiful frame from a large piece of driftwood they found on a weekend in Cambria and decorated it with sea glass she had collected along the beach. It was a few years after he passed that she got the idea to use photos that represented the elements in his tattoo and her necklace to put in it. "This only has value to me." She steadied on one shoulder with one hand while she used the other to help guide her down the ladder.

"I think it could turn out to be very valuable to me."

Sam only had a few more rungs before she reached the bottom, and she didn't have a plan.

"I see the hamster wheel in your puny little mind turning. Don't do anything stupid. Just give it to me and I'll be gone. Is it worth getting hurt over or worse?" Leticia raised the gun a little higher, emphasizing her point.

Sam's nostrils flared and muscles tensed. She wanted answers and took the next step too fast. Her foot missed the next rung. The hefty frame swayed forward. *A body in motion stays in motion.* Sam jumped off the ladder, going with the flow of the falling frame. Here was a small window of opportunity. She used the inertia of the frame and swung into Leticia, knocking her off balance and causing the gun to fly out of her hand. *Thunk!* Sam landed on her back, still gripping the frame as she gasped for the air that had just been knocked out of her. She hurried to her feet.

"You bitch!" Leticia head butted into Sam's middle, grabbing her legs, and flipping her over like a linebacker.

Sam landed hard on her back again. "Oomph!" The sharp pain in her rib cage caused her to cough and sputter as she scrambled to get up before the next blow landed. *Where is Greg, or the police, for that matter?*

"I guess it's true." Leticia circled her like a vulture. "Rich people do whatever it takes to hold on to their money."

"What are you going on about?" Sam winced as she finally got to her feet.

Leticia lifted one end of the frame. "Of course, the poor little rich girl is going to deny it."

"Oh my god, Leticia, I don't know who's been feeding you stories, but I'm not rich. You know that."

"Oh please!" She spat the words out. "You own half of a global company and a restaurant. You travel the world without a care."

"Are you kidding me!" Sam lost it. "My parents are dead, Leticia. Dead. I'd give away all my ownership, in anything, if it meant I could have them back. And as for traveling the world, I work. In every place I visit or live. I earn a living. Just like you do. No, not like you. Look how successful you are! You are a young female executive for one of the top tech companies. What could you possibly need with my picture?

What is worth killing for?" She couldn't tell if her chest hurt because of her ribs or the tears she was pushing down.

"That's a great sob story. Of course, I'm successful. I didn't really have a choice. I didn't have the-hard-working-entrepreneurial father, did I? Nooo. I had the hard-drinking father and the mother who couldn't hold a job answering phones. The only way I was going to break out of that was to climb out."

"And you did! You should be so proud of yourself! I've had...five jobs in as many years."

"Whatever, Gordon. I'm taking the picture."

Sam gazed at the framed photos. "Take it. You better hurry though, or you won't get far."

Leticia snickered. "You really don't know what's in this, do you? Your dad wasn't the saint you think he was."

"It contains memories. I'm the one who took the pictures, and my dad was exactly who I think he was!"

"It's not about the pictures." The corners of her lips curled, and her eyes glowed in the slivers of light spilling into the studio. "Why don't I just show you?"

It took a moment for Sam to register what Leticia was about to do as she watched her move closer to the counter and raise the frame over her head. "No!" Sam bolted forward, tackling Leticia sideways, and they both slammed on top of a round display table, knocking it and everything on it, including themselves, to the ground.

Sam grabbed at Leticia's ankles and got a kick to the chin before losing her grip. She scrambled to her feet, unable to see where the high school mean girl turned killer had gone.

An expletive came from the front of the studio where all the broken glass lay. Sam looked around for something to protect herself with. She spied the gun just under the stool and thought it best to avoid. *Where's the bat?* Quickly scanning the middle of the studio, she saw the bat had rolled next to the paint tube stand. Two side steps later, with bat in hand, it seemed like eons had gone by when in fact, it was probably only seconds. "So, you and Tony weren't actually dating. You met and decided to steal from my family? How does that even work?"

Silence.

She gingerly stepped around the tumbled display table craning to see behind the stack of pre-made canvases. "Poor Ms. Reed. I hate that she thinks the man she loved and was engaged to was unfaithful to her."

"Pshhh."

Sam smiled. She thought that would get a reaction and immediately moved toward the sound of the annoyed exhale. "Still, it must've been a blow to your ego that he was engaged, and with someone older than you. I mean, it's usually the other way around, isn't it?" A shuffle came from the side, but Sam was too slow to react. Leticia's hard head plowed into her ribs, and she dropped like an anchor, expelling air like a popped balloon when her back slammed into the floor. Ringing filled her ears, her head throbbed from bouncing on the floor. She couldn't determine if she was breathing or not. Sam coughed and immediately grabbed her side. Grunting, she propped herself up against the side of a supply rack. "What's your end game? You can't possibly think you're going to get away." Sam's labored breathing was starting to steady.

"I'll just carry out the original plan. Escape and all." Leticia made her way back to the frame laying cattywampus on fallen debris.

"If the plan was so good, why kill him? Did you get greedy or did Tony? Or did you find out about all of his other women and his little blackmail side hustle?" She shimmied her way up to a standing position.

"Shut up, Gordon!" Leticia bent down to get hold of the three by five-foot frame. "It's actually all your fault."

"This ought to be good. I'd never even met him." Sam rolled her eyes.

"Still. After seeing you at the party and realizing who you were... Max Gordon's baby girl all grown up. Blech! He started to have second thoughts, but I convinced him to go through with it."

While Leticia fumbled to get a good grip on the frame, Sam carefully closed the gap between them, holding in the searing pain. "Why do you think this frame is worth killing for, and if he was going through with it, why kill him?

"Your perfect father"—she grunted as she lifted the frame— "took gemstones for payment from villagers he and his team, including Tony, helped. And they are in this frame."

Sam screwed up her face, wincing as she took a step forward. "You don't think I know every inch of this frame? It's only sea glass mounted on the frame."

"They're hidden." She might as well have ended the sentence with *Duh!*

Using the bat as a cane, Sam took a couple of wobbly steps. "I don't know what Tony told you, but I promise you, there aren't any gemstones on or in that frame."

Leticia raised the frame high over her head.

Sam grabbed the bat with both hands and lunged forward, screaming out in pain as she swung the bat and swept Leticia's feet out from under her. She fell to the ground and caught a glimpse of the frame released from its captor's hands as it fell. The weight of it against the edge of the counter smashing the glass and breaking it apart. She quickly turned to protect her face from the shards flying through the air. She heard the thud of Leticia's body landing several feet away.

"Letty!" a man shouted.

He rushed past Sam, bumping her foot and crunching glass under his feet. *Who is that?* Her entire body throbbed and ached with pain. She tried to lift her head to see who it was, but another male voice came from the other direction.

"Sam?"

The lights came on, blinding her.

"Oh, geeze!" He rushed to Sam's side.

"Greg?" She squinted, trying to focus.

"I got you." He surveyed the scene. "Q's gonna kill me."

"Freeze! Police! Everyone stay where you are. Ma'am, are you okay?"

Sam was never so happy to hear Officer Riley Decker call her ma'am.

"Greg, help me up." Sam used her friend to prop her up so she could see who else had come in. She couldn't believe her eyes.

Chapter Thirty-Two

S am stared in disbelief at the sight before her. The police surrounded them. Her eyes were not playing tricks on her.

"Junior?"

His arms wrapped around Leticia's groaning body as he pressed his
cheek to hers. Sam felt like she was moving through Jell-O. Everything
was in slow motion and wobbly at the same time. Someone was asking
her a question, but she fixated on the anguished face of a man she
thought she knew.

"Miss Gordon, can I offer you some assistance?" Officer Decker
extended his hand.

"I think my rib might be broken."

"Oh my stars! Okay then, if your friend will take that side, I'll
take this side." He scooped one arm under her gluteus maximus and
the other around her back, and Greg did the same, making a human
throne. They lifted her up and set her on the stool after one of the
other officers picked it up off the floor.

Sam mumbled her thanks but didn't take her eyes of the scene in
front of her. Junior knelt next to Leticia, holding her head with one
arm and stroking her hair with his other hand.

"You're in love with her."

His head bobbed slightly.

"And you were in this together?" Sam's accusation snapped him out of it.

"No! No, Sam, not like that. No one was supposed to get hurt," Junior said.

"Why don't you tell us what it was supposed to be like." A familiar male voice came from behind her.

Sam turned to find Detective Finn standing with his arms crossed, looking very much like an unmovable statue while Junior's posture looked like a melted candle. In the time it took for her to slide off the stool, Officer Decker had Mirandized him. Wincing with each step, she asked Junior with a quiet firmness, "What was your part in all of this?"

His head made micro shakes from side to side, but he did not answer. She placed her arm on his shoulder. "Junior, please."

The long slow inhale seemed to take in the weight of the world as Junior's eyes met Sam's. "I didn't know about the heist until after ... Tony, you know."

His sad puppy dog's eyes wrenched Sam's heart, but she resisted the urge to tell him it was okay. She needed answers and nodded for him to continue.

"After I left your welcome home party, I headed to her place. I could tell how upset she was when she saw Tony with Abigail. I told her he was no good." He gestured to Sam a little too quickly for the officers' liking, and they tightened their grip on his arms. "Anyway, I thought if I could comfort her, she'd see me as more than just a friend. You know? When I pulled up to the curb, she was leaving, dressed like a ninja. So, I followed her."

Sam realized Detective Finn and Greg had moved to either side of her, listening as intently as she was.

"I couldn't figure out why she'd come back here to the studio. I thought maybe she was going to apologize, but then the lights went out and I heard a gunshot. I rushed in without thinking. It was so dark I couldn't see anything other than her"—he nodded his head to Leticia— "running out the back and then I panicked and ran. I thought for sure Joan saw my face when she came in. I called 9-1-1 the minute I got in my truck."

"Stop talking," Leticia croaked as she regained consciousness. Her words were labored as she propped herself to a seated position, her eyes darted around, seeing the broken frame.

Sam knew what she was looking for. "I told you there wasn't anything in it."

"I don't believe you. You took them while I was unconscious."

"Yes, in the split second that we all came crashing to the floor and the police and Greg came in, I managed to scramble with what I suspect is a broken rib, root around and find your gemstones and hide them." Sam tapped her shoe on part of the broken frame lying on the floor. "See. Just driftwood and sea glass."

The disbelief and confusion on Leticia's face was evident by the scowl and the hatred that emanated from her.

"You can take them away." Detective Finn nodded to Officer Decker and waved the paramedics in. "They both need to be checked." He gently touched Sam's arm. "Are you okay?"

Sam ignored her pain and knelt beside the broken frame she had made with her dad. "I'll be okay. Not so sure about this, though."

"Some resin and wood glue, and I'm sure we can fix her up, good as before," Detective Finn said.

Sam smiled through watery eyes.

Chapter Thirty-Three

The cool morning breeze wafted through Sam's hair as she strolled down the street that had been closed off to traffic for the Annual Spring Art & Craft Fair. It was hard to believe everything that happened just a week ago. She was grateful for the distraction and now the fair was moments away from officially opening, and a smattering of people had already trickled in. A smile spread across her face as she took in the colorful booths and crafty signage. She couldn't believe it all came together. Opening Aunt Lily's infamous binder, she flipped to the last tab labeled *Day Of*. Sam ran her finger down the list of tasks and found the one assigned to her. *Troubleshoot*. Next to it, a hand scrawled note read; *And enjoy!* Aunt Lily would be here soon, so a final walkthrough was in order. A gorgeous quilt caught her eye as she passed the Pieces & Patches booth. The center of the quilt was a harmonious convergence of creamy whites and delicate pinks. As the design moved outward, the colors blended into gentle lavenders and soothing purples. Continuing, the quilt's calming blues faded into emerald and spring greens, ending with hues of warm yellows, deep oranges and fiery reds blending together like a vibrant sunset.

A high-pitched female voice she recognized immediately broke Sam's reverie.

"Yoohoo!"

Sam turned to see Whiplash Whipley waving her down. "Mrs. Whipley, what can I do for you?"

"Well, there's a nail protruding from the Chamber of Commerce booth." Her hand rested on her heaving chest as she caught her breath. "Someone could cut themselves, or worse. Oh, Lily!"

"What?" Sam said confused until Mrs. Whipley pushed past her. She turned and watched as Mrs. Whipley made a beeline for Aunt Lily and Uncle Bill. *Phew, I thought one of us had just taken a hard detour from reality for a second.*

Even in a wheelchair, Aunt Lily reminded Sam of a butterfly. She wore a purple and green kaftan with billowy sleeves. Uncle Bill pushed the wheelchair and looked about to do a pop-a-wheelie when they got waylaid by Whiplash.

"Lily! Don't you look wonderful. Should you be out and about already? I can't stay and visit. I've got a minor crisis at the moment, but don't you worry, Samantha has done a stellar job." With barely a pause for breath, Whiplash Whipley patted Uncle Bill's arm and continued. "Bill, thank goodness they have a strong man like you around. I've got to dash. Don't forget about my nail, Samantha." And just like that, she was gone.

"Oh boy! She certainly lives up to her nickname." Uncle Bill gave Sam a shoulder hug, careful to avoid her still-healing ribs. "The fair looks great, kiddo."

Aunt Lily scanned the nearby booths. "Everything looks lovely, dear. You deserve a break. Give me the binder and enjoy yourself."

"I would love to get some fair food and will happily return the binder over to you. Are you sure?" Sam asked.

Uncle Bill leaned towards her. "Her pain meds will wear off in a few hours. Better take advantage now."

Sam gently set the binder in Aunt Lily's lap. "But you just go relax with Joan in the All Souls Studio booth. I can still take care of any troubleshooting."

"Nonsense, dear. I'm sure I can manage and if I need help, I'll let you know. You go on and have some fun." Aunt Lily waved her hand like a queen giving royal orders.

Bill winked at Sam as he turned to wheel Aunt Lily to her All Souls Art & Craft Studio booth.

"Will do." Sam grabbed her walkie as she took off in the opposite direction. While the art and craft displays were impressive, the best part of the fair for Sam had always been the food and she knew exactly where she wanted to start. "There's a wayward nail in Booth 109 if someone could take care of that ASAP. Please and thank you."

She didn't feel remotely self-conscious of her double order of aebleskivers, a puffy, fried dough ball coated with powdered sugar served with jammy, raspberry goodness. She popped one in her mouth and silently thanked Denmark for the scrumptious treat. The second Danish delight had a hearty dollop of jam and half of it ended up in a splatter on the ground. "Oops, maybe I shouldn't walk and eat," she said under her breath. Within moments, she found herself drawn to a booth with billows of aromatic hickory smoke filling her olfactory senses. She immediately got in line behind the only other customer. "It's never too early for BBQ," she said mostly to convince herself and anyone else in earshot, then promptly popped the only remaining aebleskiver in her mouth.

"Great minds." The customer in front of her turned around, eyes sparkling with amusement.

Sam choked on the aebleskiver she'd just put in her mouth. "Detective Finn."

"Miss Gordon." His gaze wandered to the lower half of her face.

She'd wiped her mouth with the back of her hand and created a sticky mess of jam and sugar. She plucked a handful of napkins from the dispenser on the counter. "You're out of uniform." He wore classic 501's and a faded black vintage Led Zeppelin T-shirt and she tried not to notice his biceps stretching the sleeve ever so slightly.

"I don't wear a uniform."

"You know what I mean. You are always in a suit." She finished wiping her mouth.

"What can I get you folks?" A bearded man wearing an apron covered in BBQ splatter held a pencil over a pad of paper.

"I'll have the Pig Pen," Detective Finn said.

Sam raised her hand. "Me too. I never met a pig I didn't like."

The detective grinned and nodded in agreement. "So, Miss Gordon," he began, his voice low and mischievous, "are you here on official business? Investigating the disappearance of the funnel cake recipe?"

Sam mock gasped, placing a hand over her heart. "Me? Investigate? Detective––"

"Two Pig Pens. Fifteen even." The bearded man set the food on the counter.

The detective handed him a twenty before she could lodge a protest. "Now, you were about to tell me about the break in your case." The corners of his eyes wrinkled. "And since we're at the fair and I'm off duty, you can call me Jack."

"As long as you call me Sam." She took the cardboard container he held out for her. In it was a grilled pork blend sausage in a puddle of BBQ sauced pulled pork, surrounded by thick cut steak fries. "I'm going to need more napkins. You?"

"Yup." He gave one decisive nod of his head. "Please and thank you."

"Hey, that's my line." She stepped back and pinched a handful of napkins. When she turned around, the detective motioned her to come sit on a park bench in the shade. "Would you like to eat together? *It would be awkward if we sat at different tables.* "Sure." She set the extra napkins in the center so they could share. Not exactly sure what they would talk about, she asked about Leticia's arrest.

The detective held up a finger mid-chew then swallowed. "I try not to talk shop when I'm off duty. I hope you don't mind."

"Of course. I'm so sorry. I––"

He waved her off. "No worries. That's also to let you know I won't interfere with your funnel cake investigation." He flashed a wry smile and unfurled his napkin wrapped around a fork and knife.

"Pfft! Don't worry, I'm pretty sure I've got it handled." Sam took her fork and stabbed a chubby fry, scooping up a clump of pulled pork and sauce and landed it in her watering mouth. Her eyes rolled up involuntarily.

"That good, huh?"

She chuckled, slightly embarrassed. She watched as he took his first bite. A smile spread across his face as he chewed. "Well?"

The detective smacked his lips, then dabbed it with a napkin. "You didn't exaggerate." He picked up a fry and swirled it in the BBQ sauce. "So, will you be going back to England soon?"

She paused, her fork mid-air. Tilting her head, her eyes looked up as if the answer was in a corner of her brain. "You know, I think I've decided to stick around."

"Interesting."

Sam wasn't sure what to make of his comment. "Is that good, interesting or bad interesting?" Her brows raised.

"No, no. I'm just surprised. I bet your aunt is happy you're staying."

"She will be once I tell her. And don't worry, I'll do a better job keeping you informed of any clues the next time a case comes up."

The detective coughed and sputtered. "Next time?"

"Oh, my gosh!" Sam patted his back. "Are you okay?" She couldn't tell if he was nodding yes or if his head was bobbing because of the coughing.

The walkie-talkie squawked. "Sam, we have a situation at the Catopia booth." It was Trent, one of the high school's Future Business Leaders volunteers. "It's kind of an emergency. Oh, and you might want to bring gloves."

"I've got to go." She swiped a napkin over her fingers and gazed forlornly at the unfinished meal.

The detective drank water, trying to gain his composure from choking a mere moment ago, nodded and held his hand up to wave goodbye.

"Thanks so much for the BBQ! Next one's on me."

Sam sprinted to the Catopia Cat Café booth, clutching the oven mitts she borrowed from the baking supply store booth, Whisk Me Away. She skidded to a halt when she saw the commotion. A crowd of people had gathered around the booth, pointing and laughing. Sam pushed her way through and spotted Mrs. Whipley, who was shrieking and flailing her arms. An orange tabby kitten clung to her bouffant hairdo for dear life.

"Get it off me! Get it off!"

The kitten let out a high-pitched sorrowful mew that matched Mrs. Whipley's screams.

"Mrs. Whipley, it's just a kitten. It's more scared than you are." Sam moved closer, sliding the mitts on.

"I doubt that! Do something, Samantha!" Mrs. Whipley screamed, spinning around, and knocking over a display of cat toys. She lost her balance the same moment Detective Finn broke through the crowd, and she fell into the detective. They were both going down like a sack of potatoes.

Sam shoved a bale of hay as hard as she could. It couldn't have worked better than if it had been a coordinated stunt. The detective landed in an almost seated position on the bale of hay. Mrs. Whipley landed somewhat awkwardly in his lap.

"I've got you ma'am." The detective helped Mrs. Whipley to her feet.

Whiplash Whipley fluttered. "Oh, my you certainly do." She straightened her skirt the mewling kitten nearly forgotten.

Sam moved right next to Mrs. Whipley and spoke in a low, smooth tone. She wasn't sure if it was to calm Whiplash or the kitten. "Please stay calm. I'm just going to..." She reached up to grab the scared kitten, who immediately hissed and tried to swipe at her. Thank goodness for the oven mitts. Gently wrapping them around the kitten, she lifted the kitten off Mrs. Whipley's head, except several of the tabby's claws were tangled in the teased bouffant hair. She looked to the detective, who bit down on his lip stifling a smile. Sam raised a brow that successfully conveyed *A little help, please!*

He quickly took hold of her elbow. "Here. Why don't you sit down."

"Such a gentleman." Mrs. Whipley sat gazing at the detective.

Sam carefully untangled the kitten's claws from the teased and overly sprayed bouffant. Although now Mrs. Whipley's hair-do looked like a deflated soufflé, the kitten was free. It wiggled and leaped

out of Sam's mitts and onto the detective's shoulder, where it promptly nuzzled his neck.

"Looks like someone has found their forever home," Sam teased.
She didn't have enough time to process the other thoughts she was
having.

The walkie talkie sounded. Another young volunteer spoke. "Sam,
we need you at the Clay Mates booth right away! Bring a bucket of
water and towels. Oh! And maybe a couple of those drywall scraper
things." She didn't even want to think about the kind of mess the
pottery wheel could have created.

***

The sun hung low, casting a golden light over the fair. As the event
wound down, the streets cleared. The last few people who lingered
enjoyed their food and showed each other the items they'd purchased.

Sam entered the Café Nate booth and slumped into a folding chair
in the mini dining area. She checked her watch, quarter after six. "Darn
it," and pressed the talk button on the walkie. "Edith, we need to close
up the entrance."

"Already done, dearie."

Sam could hear the pride in Edith's voice. "You're the best! Thank
you, Edith." She took in a slow, deep breath and let out a heavy sigh of
satisfaction, then emptied her pockets onto the table in front of her.

"What's all this?" Q asked, appearing from the temporary kitchen
behind the curtain.

"I'm trying to find—here it is." She triumphantly held up a small
clear tube with pale pink inside it. "My lip gloss!" She swiped the gloss
around her lips. "Am I smelling bacon?"

"Are you hungry? I'm making myself breakfast for dinner. I figure I'd better eat now because it'll be too late by the time I pack up and get home."

Sam's stomach answered before she could. "Yes please! It's been bananas. Every time I thought I was going to eat something, a crisis popped up."

Q disappeared behind the curtain and reappeared just a few moments later with two plates and two red plastic cups. "I brought some iced tea."

Sam reached for the plates Q was balancing on her forearms. "I don't know how you do that." On the plate were four slices of extra crispy bacon, dark golden hash browns, two eggs over hard and a slice of well-buttered sourdough toast.

Q moved the multi-colored sea glass around with her finger. "Wouldn't it be bizarre if these were real gemstones?" She held up a pale-colored piece of sea glass, turning it to catch the light. "Like, what if this was really a diamond or something?"

Sam chuckled. "Yeah right. Here, pass that over." She took the sea glass from Q and rolled it between her fingers. "A genuine diamond would cut this." Casually, she dragged it across the surface of her small round pocket mirror. It left a scratch in its wake.

"See?" She rubbed her finger across it to make her point. "Ouch!"

Transfixed by the growing red droplet on her finger, Sam slowly looked up at Q, then back down at the stone in her hand. She blinked once, then twice as the implications sunk in. No words were needed - the looks on their faces said it all.

Chapter Thirty-Four

The End of Book 1

If you enjoyed this book, please consider leaving a review. And if you want to be notified when Sam has her next adventure, *Unpacking Murder*, join my newsletter at www.anneseidelauthor.com

About the Author

Anne Seidel is a Southern California native, currently living in the heart of Orange County, and frequently watches fireworks from the "Happiest Place on Earth", through her home office window. Her love of mysteries started with Saturday morning cartoon sleuths. Though she has just recently started her publishing journey, there is no lack of mysteries brewing in her brain for Sam Gordon Mysteries and is eager to share them with you. When she's not plotting a murder mystery, she loves a good road trip. Of course what better inspiration than a long lonely highway, whether it's here in the states or driving on the "wrong" side of the road in the UK, Anne gets inspiration from just about anywhere, anything, anytime.

Follow her and Sam as they head toward their next adventure by signing up for her monthly Anne-A-Gram newsletter for news and special offers. Or visit her at www.anneseidelauthor.com

Made in the USA
Monee, IL
05 October 2023